I0591461

HE IS
OURS
Rebekah Lynn

Copyright © 2025 by Rebekah Lynn

All rights reserved.

No part of this publication may be reproduced, distributed, or transmitted
in any form or by any means, including photocopying, recording, or other
electronic or mechanical methods, without the prior written permission
of the publisher, except as permitted by U.S. copyright law. For permission
requests, contact Rebekah Lynn

The story, all names, characters, and incidents portrayed in this production
are fictitious. No identification with actual persons (living or deceased),
places, buildings, and products is intended or should be inferred.

Book Cover by Rebekah Lynn

Illustrations by Rebekah Lynn

1st edition 2025

For the ones who love the monsters they should fear, and for the monsters who will burn the world for them. This one is for you.

~Rebekah

Trigger Warnings

He Is Ours explores themes of heavy content, including but not limited to:

- Human Auction

- Sexual activity

- Death

- Graphic scenes

- Guns

- Shooting

- Human trafficking

- Mental Trauma

- Kidnapping

- Mild BDSM

- Death threats

- Pregnancy

- Torture

- Underground fighting

- Gambling

- Anxiety attacks

- PTSD

Playlist

All of Me by John Legend
Stay With Me by Sam Smith
Thinking out Loud by Ed Sheeran
Say You Won't Let Go by James Arthur
Just Give Me a Reason by P!nk, Nate Ruess
I'm Yours by Jason Mraz
i wanna be your slave by Mitchell Zia
Marry Me by Jason Derulo
Animal I Have Become by Three Days Grace
Dirty Thoughts by Chloe Adams
Take Me Away by New Medicine
Fine by Kyle Hume
Devil in Her Eyes by Bryce Savage
Trainwreck by Ryan Jesse
No Mercy by Austin Giorgio
keep your demons by TAELA
Control by Bryce Savage
Ordinary by Alex Warren

Chapter One

Rachel

I am in this banquet hall; don't get me wrong, it's beautiful. The decorations are incredible, but looking around at all these entitled rich fucks who want to buy humans, these people make me sick. If I could kill them all, I would. Alex and I stay in the shadows until it's time for action. Alex told us generally what was going to happen. Unfortunately, our plan won't go into action until Olivia has been completely exposed. Alex says he knows his grandfather can't resist a ridiculously high bid, so when the bidding starts, he will let it play out a little bit, and then he will make a ridiculous offer to win Olivia

I see my girl sitting in a chair near the stage, looking as if scanning the area thoroughly. She looks absolutely stunning tonight. Her auburn hair is curled and falling down her back. She is wearing an emerald dress that complements her pale skin to perfection. Her makeup is subtle but makes her blue/green eyes pop, and her lips look kissable, just as I like them. But in reality, Olivia is the only girl I have wanted. Before her, I had never been attracted to a woman at all. But something about Olivia has captured me like a moth to a flame.

I didn't realize how quickly I could care for someone either, but all it took was one night with her, followed by losing her, to know that I wanted to try my hardest to make this work. I want her and Alex. I don't understand it, but it's what I feel. After everything with Andrew, you don't want to pass up perfection when you see it in the flesh.

"Good evening, everyone." An older man who resembles an older version of Alex says this into a microphone on the stage, grabbing everyone's attention.

"Tonight is a very special night, and I have a surprise in store for you," he says.

The chatter starts to rumble through the crowd.

"What surprise?" A man next to me says.

"I wonder what it could be?" Another lady whispers.

I look at Alex and cock a brow, but he shrugs his shoulders. I would have thought he would have known.

We are almost certain that Olivia will be up for auction tonight. The intel we received from Oliver's team, combined with what Alex could gather from his grandfather's team, led us to this assumption.

"Usually, my annual auctions are a little more of the mixed variety, if you know what I mean." Alex's grandfather says. The crowd around us gives a small chuckle at his words, and I roll my eyes. Mixed variety... Fucking gross. This man gives me all the creeps. I feel like I need to take a shower just after being around these fuckers.

Alex puts his hand on my lower back to calm me down. Given everything we had learned, he knows how worked up I am right now.

"But this year, not only will I have the usual product up for auction, but I also have a beautiful woman who is quite unique up for auction tonight as well." *My fucking woman*, I wanted to yell at him. I wanted to go up knives swinging and demand that he hand her over. How dare he take what is mine!

But I have to keep my cool. We have a plan; if I let my hot-headedness get the best of me, I will ruin it all and possibly get us killed in the process.

I see four men in suits walk up behind Olivia, who is seated in her chair. One grabs her, pulls her up, and wraps his arms around her. She starts to kick and scream, and it breaks my heart.

"Tony, Stop! Get your hands off of me!" I hear her yell. The sound of fear in her voice causes my heart to strain and my blood to boil. She sounds so hopeless in that yell.

Tony.

Noted.

Tony, you are mine! You will be my kill tonight, mark my fucking words!

I grab Alex's arm and pull him down to me while he watches Olivia in horror.

"I want that Tony fucker! You can kill anyone else, but Tony is mine." I am stern, with no room for argument. The fire in my blood is screaming for revenge.

"Ok, babe. He is yours. But we have to wait until it's time." I nod at him. I know I have to wait, but I don't have to like it.

"She is a feisty one." The dark-haired man next to me says. My hands ball into fists, so tight that my nails are cutting into my skin. I want to punch him in the face!

"I wouldn't mind a piece of that." The lady in the blue dress with her brown hair pinned up on the top of her head, holding onto a blonde-haired man's arm, says.

"I wish Lopez always brought these types of women instead of the ugly ones and kids; I would buy more often, " a short, bald man in front of us says.

All these comments make me murderous. As if I weren't barely holding on already, I would be now. These fuckers are nasty!

Tony gets Olivia on stage, and you can see the pure terror on her face. Alex's grandfather leans down and talks to Olivia, and so does that fucker Tony. After whatever they say, Olivia becomes even paler in the face.

"Let's get this show on the road, shall we?" Booms through the speakers around the room, and you can feel the excitement buzzing through the room. Olivia looks at Grandpappy like he has lost his damn mind. Because obviously, he has!

I see Olivia moving up on stage some more, wiggling like she is trying to get out of Tony's grip, and then another big man in a tux, just like the other security personnel—if you can even call them that—grabs Olivia's wrist to put handcuffs on her. He bends down and whispers something into her ear. She turns to look at him and then at Tony, who hasn't stopped glaring at her.

They get Olivia to the center of the stage, the light shining directly on her. Even as terrified as I know she is, she still looks absolutely beautiful up there. I fucking hate that the circumstances are shitty because I just want to devour her with my eyes!

"Well, Ladies and Gentlemen. That was a bit dramatic. I apologize for that. This here is Olivia. Not only can you tell that she is a fiery redhead, but she is also a dear Irish Mafia Princess. Her family is the O'Connor family in New York; they hold the biggest gun trading on the East Coast." Grandpappy says.

Wait a fucking minute! Mafia Princess? What the fuck am I missing?

"Did you know she was a part of the mafia?" I whisper to Alex. He slowly nods his head. The anger was rising in me. I turn to face him now. "You knew, and you didn't tell me? What the fuck, Alex!" My voice raised just a smidge more, but not enough for anyone else to hear me.

"Rachel, stop. We can talk about this later." His words are like nails on a chalkboard to me. Fucker telling me to stop.

"Don't you fucking..." My anger outburst was cut off by fucking Grandpappy talking about my woman.

"She sits five feet five inches tall and is a solid one hundred and twenty pounds, not an ounce of fat on this woman, ladies and gentlemen. She works for the San Diego Police Department. So, as you can see, our little mafia princess is straddling both sides of the law. Imagine what else she could be straddling." He says with a chuckle, and the whole room chuckles and murmurs their agreement to his stupid comment. My molars are grinding in the back of my mouth, and I will be surprised if I don't chip a tooth. My fucking whole body is so taught, I am like a bow string ready to release this anger.

"I can't wait until they strip her," one of the people behind me says, and I am seeing black. I feel Alex's hand wrap around my waist and tighten his grip just to keep me put. He can sense the rage within me.

I can't ruin the plan.
I can't ruin the plan.
I can't ruin the plan.

I keep chanting in my head so I will hopefully calm down. Fun fact for the day—it's not helping.

"Ok, now for the good parts." Ugh, his voice buzzing in my ears, sharp and relentless, like a swarm of angry wasps.

Grandpappy grabs Olivia by the arm and spins her around, making her face Tony. I see her knee make contact with his balls. He didn't even fucking flinch. Does he even have balls?

Grandpappy grabs the bottom of Olivia's dress and tries to pull it up, not bothering with the zipper in the back of the beautiful gown. When it stops mid-thigh, you can see him lean towards Olivia's ear and whisper something. When Grandpappy stands back up, Tony reaches for his belt, grabs the knife that was holstered, and points it toward Olivia. He grabs the top of her dress and starts to cut down the center between her breasts! I swear to fucking god, he better not cut her perfect breasts, or I'm going to skin him alive! I will make it the slowest and most painful death anyone has seen.

I see blood trickling down Olivia's wrists, and she yells out, "No! Stop!" She starts to move so they can't cut the dress. Rage now takes over in Grandpappy and Tony's eyes. When they get a glimpse of what is going on, I see the cut from Olivia's sternum to her stomach. White, hot boiling rage runs through my veins.

They fucking cut her. He marked my beautiful woman's body with a knife.

"Look what you did, you fucking stupid girl!" Grandpappy growls in her face and then slaps her across the face. Every time they hit her or mark her, that is another stab wound I will happily inflict on them, causing him the most pain but not enough to kill him quickly.

I look back up just in time to see my girl turn and spit in his face! Blood and spit traced a slow, glistening path down his cheek. He wipes the liquid off his face, and the smile on his face turns pure evil. He grabs the two halves of her dress, rips it entirely in half, and throws it to the side. Now, Olivia stands there in nothing but sparkly jewelry and black heels.

"Alright, ladies and gentlemen, the last of the viewing before we start the bidding." It breaks my heart to look at Olivia nude in front of all of these people. I want to rip out everyone's eyeballs just for looking at her.

Tony pushes Olivia down so she bends at the waist and kicks her legs open so that everyone can have a perfect look at her pussy and ass. That beautiful body that belongs to me is on full display for the whole world to see.

Comments are coming from all around the room about her, and it takes every ounce of self-control I have to not freak the fuck out and make a blood bath of this ballroom.

"Look at that pussy. It looks tight as fuck."

"She is a brat that I would like to get hold of."

"I wonder what all she has done with her tight ass."

Tony lifted her back up and turned her around to show everyone her front. You can see the long cut on her breasts from when she tried to fight Tony, and now that I have seen it with my own two eyes, I will skin Tony alive!

"She has some nice tits!" A blonde girl says in front.

"Can we start the bidding already?" The guy behind me says. He has had a comment for everything tonight. If I didn't have my eyes set on killing Tony, that guy would be dead.

"Alright, ladies and gentlemen, we will start the bidding at thirty-five thousand dollars. Do I hear someone for thirty-five?" Grandpappy starts the bidding.

"Thirty-five," a guy in the front says, raising his auction paddle with the number 165 on it.

"Forty," I hear from a female behind me.

"Fifty," I hear another female say further to the left of us.

The bids keep coming from every direction. The price is rising and rising. We are sitting at three hundred and fifty thousand dollars.

"Alex, Fucking do something!" I exclaim. I am start-ing to panic. The bids getting this high were not a part of the plan.

"One million dollars," Alex yells over the crowd, hold-ing up his auction paddle with the number 210 on it. My jaw dropped. One million fucking dollars? Does Alex even have that kind of money? I mean, his grandfather is the Drug Lord of the cartel, so I guess they do have money, but still, one million?

"SOLD! For One Million Dollars to the gentleman in the back!" Grandpappy yells into the microphone with too much excitement in his voice.

Tony starts to drag Olivia off the stage, and I start to freak out.

I grab Alex's hand and start to walk toward the stage. "They can't take her, Alex. We need to get to her! What if they realize it's you and take her?" I am babbling all of my concerns out right now, and Alex is calm, cool, and collected.

"She comes with me!" Alex yells, and Tony stops dead in his tracks and turns with fire in his eyes.

When Olivia finally realizes it's us running up to the stage, her eyes go big with hurt and longing, but then it turns straight to rage. I don't know why she is mad, but I can figure that out later.

Chapter Two

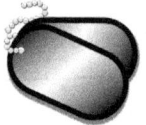

Alex

Before I can even process anything in my brain, I am running towards the stage. The only coherent thought in my mind is that I need to get to Olivia as fast as possible. Rachel is right behind me, not missing a step. We are both trying to get our girl out of the slimy grip of Tony and my Grandfather.

When we finally get to the stage, I see the guy behind Tony. A bullet tore through his temple, and for a second, he just stood there, eyes wide with shock, before his knees buckled and he dropped to the ground. The guy behind my grandfather drops next—a bullet to the chest, blood pooling under his lifeless body.

Damn! Oliver is a good shot.

I pull out my gun and turn, pointing it at my grandfather at the same time as Rachel has her knives out, spinning them in her hands like a show-off. She prefers to stab or slice someone, but she also has a good aim with throwing. I'm just grateful I got the target at home to start throwing at to practice.

As soon as everyone finally takes notice that the people lying on the ground are actually dead, blood-curdling screams start to erupt, and everyone starts to run in panic for the doors.

A smile forms on my face when I see my grandfather's jaw tighten and his nostrils flare. His narrow eyes turn towards me, screaming that he is losing his patience. Tony - my grandfather's puppet - is looking around for the source of the bullet that has claimed residency in his two men, who are now staining the pristine floor.

If everything goes according to plan, Oliver will already be hiding somewhere on the second floor. I gave him a quick rundown of the floor plans before we got here, so he knew the best hiding places. I was a kid raised here by Satan himself. If anyone knows the best hiding spots, it would be me. But I do have to give my grandfather the benefit of the doubt; of all the places to hold my girl hostage, had his wicked ways with her, and bid her off, the home I grew up in was not one of my top choices. This place is full of the ghosts of my past that I never wanted to face again, but here I am, facing every single one of them, while I still need to keep my composure for both of these women who need me.

He outsmarted me, hiding her in plain sight. God, I can't get over that. Why didn't I think of it... This will eat at me for the rest of my life. I could have saved Olivia from a world of pain, torture, and trauma. I was thinking of every other place he might take her to, and I found out that Oliver's men were on the right track the whole time.

"Give me Olivia, now!" I shouted. He gives Olivia a slight tilt of his head and then slowly extends his hand, palm up, towards the ceiling, flicking his fingers towards me to encourage Olivia to come to me, but she doesn't move. She stands slightly behind Tony, almost as if she were cowering behind him. The look in her eyes, wide, wary, like I am now a stranger to her, cut me deeper than any other wound I have had.

I am on the stage within three steps, grabbing Olivia from Tony's reach. Her look now morphed into pure terror when she noticed my hand on her arm. Her eyes are now impossibly wide, whites showing all around her irises. Her mouth is slightly open, like she wants to scream. Her lips were trembling as if no words were able to come out, and only panic remained in her body.

What the fuck did my grandfather tell her?

Why is she so afraid of me?

I take off my leather jacket and drape it around her to cover her still-naked body, only for her to shrug it off and rip her arm out of my hand. "Don't you dare fucking touch me!" She yells at me. My grandfather's laughter booms through the room. He is enjoying this show.

"What? She doesn't want you now. Poor Alejandro. Always the hero who came to the rescue too late." I turn towards him, shooting him a look that could burn a damn hole through steel. I swear to fucking god I will kill him, regardless of us sharing the same blood.

"What did you tell her?" I run up to him, grabbing him by the collar of his button-up white shirt, my gun pressed up tight against his temple, ready to shoot his brains out with one wrong move.

"I didn't tell her anything but the truth, my dear grandson." The slimy smile on his face makes my stomach turn; I know he said something to fuck with Olivia's head.

Rachel is physically shaking with anger next to me. Her hands are wrapped around her knives so tightly that her knuckles are turning red, and her eyes are zoned in on Tony. I know she is analyzing every slice and stab that will be inflicted on his body by her hands.

I approach my grandfather, hand him the check that I wrote out for a million dollars for Olivia, and turn, not giving him a second glance. I walk up to Olivia and reach out my hand to take hers, and she flinches, the flash of betrayal written all over her face.

"I. SAID. DON'T. TOUCH. ME!" Every word she spat out had venom dripping off it. This is not *my Olivia*.

She turns towards Tony and starts to walk towards the back of the stage. Tony shoots a victorious look over his shoulder at me, and my blood boils. He thinks he has won, but little does he know he has won a one-way ticket to hell. By the end of the night, he will be six feet under at the hands of a crazy blonde who wants her woman back. Eventually, I will meet him there and continue to make him pay for the disgusting and vile things he did to Olivia.

From the corner of my eye, I see Rachel start to stalk towards him. When she gets close enough, she pulls up her dress, jumps on Tony's back, and digs the heel of her red stilettos into his calf to climb higher on his back. When she finally gets in the position she wants, she wraps her legs around his waist and swings her knife through the air, stabbing his right shoulder first, making sure to twist it and pull it to tear the muscles. Tony roars out in pain as Olivia watches Rachel with a mix of horror and surprise in her eyes. I forgot; she doesn't know that Rachel killed Andrew or had an obsession with knives. When Rachel pulls the knife out, she stabs Tony's other shoulder, making sure to dig the blade in deep.

"Get off me bitch!" Tony tries to swing, turn, and buck Rachel off of him, but she is holding on tight, not letting anything get her off his back. The thrill in her eyes is shining bright as she rides Tony like a bull at a rodeo. I even think I heard her yeehaw at one point. I just stand back and cross my arms, watching my woman with pride and love in my eyes.

Rachel jumps off of Tony's back after the short bucking ride, ducking under his arm as he swings out to hit her. She takes the opening and stabs him in the stomach next, and then turns her head towards his ear. "I don't fucking think so fucker! You took what was mine! You hurt what was mine! You used what was mine! And now you will fucking pay!"

She stabs him in the stomach three more times and once in each eye before she jumps back and watches him crumble to the floor. Her pupils are blown wide with fury, and her stare is as sharp as the dagger in her hand that is dripping with Tony's blood.

She steps back and finally turns towards Olivia, desperation, longing, love, and raw pain drowning out every other emotion in her bright blue eyes.

"Olivia, are you ok?" She whispers. The question was rhetorical, but I knew she needed to hear Olivia's voice. The adrenaline was still coursing through her veins as she tried to make a connection with Olivia and let her know that we were on her side, that we loved her, and that we needed her now more than ever.

The terror in Olivia's eyes as she stared at Rachel for a long minute was so stark, so overwhelming, that it shattered my heart into a million jagged pieces.

"Olivia? Come here, baby... Please." Rachel's voice is broken and needy as she walks up, arms wide, to Olivia. Olivia's eyes widen, and she steps back, bumping into Tony's lifeless body on the ground, blood pooling around him, unconscious from blood loss. She looks down in horror at Tony, back up to Rachel, and then around the room for an escape.

"Olivia? What's going on, baby? Talk to me." You can hear the desperation in Rachel's voice. I see her heart breaking with every word that leaves her mouth; she just wants Olivia to say anything to her, to know *our Olivia* is still in there.

Olivia stares at Rachel with a blank look. Her once-blue-green eyes are now a grey color, almost as lifeless as the dead men behind her. I don't know what she went through or what is going on in her head, but I need to find out. I need to handle this situation with care and get her home safely. I need to heal the pieces my Grandfather broke.

Olivia looks at me, then back at Rachel. You can see the wheels turning in her head as she figures out what to do next. Her eyes look from us to the door in the back of the banquet hall several times, then she turns on her heels and runs down the stairs, heading straight toward the back door. I saw her looking around for an exit before the auction happened, but she didn't know the house well enough to know which door was the exit. Rachel starts to run after her, and I grab her wrist to stop her. Only one person can handle this, so I do the only thing that comes to mind. I pull out my phone and call Oliver.

I hear him answer the phone, but he doesn't say anything.

"Your sister is heading your way. Go down the stairs, and she should run into you. She is scared, and she doesn't trust me or Rachel. I think you are the only one she will trust right now." I hang up the phone and hear fast, loud, heavy footsteps from above, and I know it's Oliver going after Olivia. If there is one person she feels safe with, it will be her twin.

I turn and look at the podium to find my grandfather no longer standing there. Of course, he ran; the man is a coward, never in the action, and never takes accountability for his actions. But that's ok. I will hunt him down. I will go to every corner of the world to find him and kill him with my bare hands.

I turn to Rachel and see her looking at Tony, studying his now dead body, with tears streaming down her face. I hate when these girls cry; it breaks my fucking heart.

"Hey, what's wrong?" I hold her face in my hands and wipe her tears off her cheeks with my thumbs.

"It breaks my fucking heart, Alex. They fucking took the light out of her. They took everything good out of her. She is now a shell of a person. Will we be able to get her back? She is fucking scared of us. What do we do? I don't think I can live without her."

"I did what we could. They got into her head. I don't know what they said, but I will find out. But right now, I have to trust that Oliver will be able to bring her back to us. He has to help calm her down, and then maybe we can talk to her. If she will open up to anyone, it's him." She nods in response, and I wrap her in a hug, burying my nose into her hair, smelling her floral shampoo.

I have to give Oliver time, I remind myself. I know he knows what he is doing. I grab Rachel's hand and intertwine my fingers with hers.

"Let's go see our girl." I bend down, kiss the top of Rachel's head, and head towards the double doors in the back.

Chapter Three

Olivia

Everything is happening too fast. My brain is swimming in pure terror. I was just sold. Fucking sold like cattle. And of all the people to buy me, it was Alex!

That fucker just bought me!

I didn't want to believe he was like his grandfather, but now he's proven it.

The Lopez García men—*they're all the same. MONSTERS!*

I run out of the double doors at the back of the banquet hall. My heart is pounding, my breath ragged, but I can't stop running, not now. I don't know where I'm going, but I know I have to get away—away from Alex, away from Lopez García, away from all of it. The walls feel like they are closing in on me. I can't breathe, and my heart is pounding out of my chest. I don't know who I can trust anymore, and that makes my head start to spin.

I need time, time to think, process, and try to become human again. My thoughts are everywhere. Maybe I'll get on a plane and go to New York, to our family's house. No one knows where I'm from, and Oliver and Dad will make sure no one gets on the property. But even that thought feels too easy; I can't escape just by running. Alex would find me; I know he would. Plus, I wasn't raised to be a coward.

The way Alex looked at me when I was sold—like he had every right to own me. That look is burned into my mind for the rest of my life. How could I have trusted him so much? How could I have been so blind? The only other time I have seen that look is when we were having sex. It was pure ownership in his eyes. Did he want to save me? Or is he just keeping what he thinks is his?

I turn a corner, lost in my thoughts, and run straight into a hard chest. I fall backward onto the floor with an oomph. The cold tile under my palms caused my wrist to ache from the impact. When I look up, I see the one person I wasn't expecting to be there.

Oliver.

I blink rapidly, my breath catching in my throat. I want to make sure I am not hallucinating. I should feel safe, but I don't. I don't know how to put it into words. It feels like another puzzle piece that doesn't quite fit right. What's he doing here? I want to reach for him, hug him, cry on his chest, but there's this knot in my stomach that is stopping me. Do I trust him? Can I? I've known him my whole life. For fuck sake, we shared a damn womb together, but right now, everything feels like a lie.

"Oliver? Is that really you?" My voice trembles, and I can't help it. I'm scared. Scared of what I feel and scared of what's coming, scared this is just one big nightmare, and I am still stuck in that stupid basement.

He opens his mouth to say something, then closes it again. That tiny hesitation hits harder than any words could. When the words finally come out, they are hushed. "Yeah, Livy. It's me. I'm here." His arms are open, but instead of running into them like I've done my whole life, I hesitate, as if I'm waiting for a trap to spring into action, the other shoe to drop.

When I finally get the courage to walk into his arms, the sobs come out of me instantly, uncontrollably. The weight of everything crashes down on me: Alex, Lopez García, being sold, the fear, the uncertainty, even seeing Rachel kill Tony. I cry like I've never cried before, my body shaking against his. As much as I need him, there's this gnawing feeling at the back of my mind that won't let me fully let go.

"Why are you here?" The question slips out before I can stop it. I realize the underlying question I am really asking: Tell me I can trust you, Oliver. Fucking Lie to me if you have to. I just need something to believe in right now.

He runs a hand down his face like he's hiding something, and I don't like it. I don't like that nervous tick of his. It's a sign. A sign that something's off.

"Oliver, what the fuck is going on? Why are you here?" I pull away, eyes narrowed in question. Every part of me screams for answers, but now my heart is pounding in a different way—*fear*. I fear that the one person I've trusted more than anyone in this world might be lying to me, also.

Oliver sighs, rubbing his arm, and I see it—the nervousness growing in his eyes. He knows something I don't.

"Alex called me," he finally says, his voice low. "He told me his grandfather had you. We came up with a plan to get you out and bring you home."

The world tilts beneath me, and I grab the wall for support. Alex? The man who helped lock me in this hellhole, the man who's part of the very family I've been running from?

Why would he care now? Why is Oliver working with him?

My head is spinning again, and I can't make sense of any of this. Who's telling the truth? Who's lying to me?

And then there's Rachel; where does she fit into all of this?

I force myself to breathe, but it feels like my lungs are caving in. Can I trust my twin?

Oliver notices my brain is going a thousand miles an hour and gently grabs my face, making me look at him. "Livy, breathe for me." I hadn't realized I'd been holding my breath, but of course, he would know. He always knows. Will I also regret trusting you? The thought comes as a shock to me as I try to take deep breaths.

Why wouldn't I trust my twin?

Probably because he withheld my whole family's business from me for years?

The internal battle I am having is causing me to feel like I am insane.

I nod weakly, letting out the breath slowly and sinking into his chest. At this moment, I can't think straight. All I can feel is his steady heartbeat against my cheek. It's familiar and comforting, and even though every instinct tells me to question everything, I keep my head on Oliver's chest, listening to his heart and smelling his shirt. It smells just like I remember.

"Hey, Oli... can you please take me back to my house?" The words come out soft as I look up at him. I need to be somewhere safe, somewhere I can think. Somewhere without all the lies. He nods and pulls me close, wrapping his arms around my shoulder.

I feel him glance over his shoulder; I can't help but wonder—What's behind us? What did he see that I missed?

I want to question him, but I don't have the energy to care right now. I just want to leave this hellhole and never look back.

Chapter Four

Rachel

Oliver turns and mouths something to Alex, but I can't tear my gaze away from Olivia walking away to care about what they are talking about. I don't know how to fix this. I don't know what to do to make her believe me, to understand that we had nothing to do with this, that all we want is for her to be back home with us. My head is spinning with ideas as my hands are clenched around the hilt of my knives, and the anger starts to rise.

This is not how tonight was supposed to go!

It was supposed to end with Alex and me as the superheroes, saving the day and making everything right. And now... now I don't even get to be the hero who saves the girl and lives happily ever after. Instead, the villain in me is showing her face, and the need to make someone pay is undeniable.

The anger burns through me, a fire demanding retribution. What they did to Olivia... It crossed a line. And there's no turning back now. They *will* face the consequences. Every second that ticks by fuels the urge to make them understand the cost of their actions. It's not just about making things right anymore; It's about making them suffer for messing with what is mine!

No one messes with what is mine and lives to tell about it.

They destroyed her and took her beautiful light from her soul. I will destroy them in the most brutal way possible. Mark my words.

I turn around on my heels and start to walk away when a hand wraps around my arm to stop me.

"Where are you going?" Alex's voice is strained as he tries to pull me into a hug. But I shrug him off, shoving him away from me.

"I'm sorry, I can't right now." I snap, the words sharp with venom. "I am pissed, and someone needs to pay. I am going to find every mother fucker involved and make them all suffer. They will be hoping and praying for death by the time I am done with them."

lex raises an eyebrow; his gaze is unreadable, but he doesn't stop me. Instead, he lets me walk away.

I walk back into the banquet hall, my eyes scanning the room. Everyone's gone except the dead, fucking cowards. Everyone runs as soon as someone dies, but they are willing to buy a human for their own selfish needs.

One body lies still, his eyes wide open, staring blankly at the ceiling. A single bullet hole deep into his skull, dark blood dripping down his forehead, pooling beneath his head.

The second man is no better. Lifeless. Another bullet wound, but this one in the chest. His blood stains the fabric of his white button-up shirt.

And then there's Tony. Fucking Tony. He's clutching his stomach, his face frozen in terror, eyes wide with the realization of his demise. Dark and thick blood is still fresh beneath him, pooling around his body in glistening rivers.

The stench of death hangs in the air, choking me, but it only pushes me further. Every one of these bastards deserved their end. The guests? Lucky for them, they weren't on my hit list... but their time will come, too. I can promise you that. When I am done, there will be no one to purchase humans, so that the skin trade will die.

I kneel by Tony's lifeless body and search his suit for anything helpful—anything that might help me track down Lopez García, or that could help me get Olivia back. At this point, I'll grasp at any shred of hope.

My fingers brush against something hard— a knife. I pull it free from its sheath and inspect it carefully. The handle is bone, off-white, with intricate carvings—a name etched into it: Sanchez. The blade is made of Damascus steel, glimmering with beautiful, wave-like patterns that almost remind me of water ripples. It's heavy, and it feels... perfect. The weight of it is comforting, almost like an extension of myself.

I carefully slip the blade back into its sheath, tucking it into my cleavage for safekeeping while I continue my search. Nothing else stands out to me, just a standard-issued 9mm pistol and a wallet.

I checked the other two men. It's the same deal. Just 9mm and wallets; fucking boring. Nothing is worth my time except for this knife. This knife gives me a small glimmer of hope that we will find Lopez García and make the world right again.

I find Alex still standing in the hallway, staring at the spot where Olivia and Oliver were as if lost. His face is a mix of confusion and loss, and it breaks my heart. I just want to take away his pain, but I can't. I am fucking done with not being able to help.

I stood there for another couple of minutes, finally becoming irritated with his pouting. I march to him, "Are we going to stand here and sulk? Or are we going to get our girl? I'm done with this fucking house. And frankly, I have so much rage right now; I need to get it out before I explode."

Alex blinks, snapping out of his daze, and looks down to meet my gaze.

"Let's go home and figure out how to get our girl back."

I grab his hand and pull him out of the house towards the 4Runner. I am getting my girl back, with or without

Alex. Olivia has made me feel things I have never felt before, and I refuse to lose that. Olivia treats me just like her nickname for me -princess- she worships the ground I walk on. I have never had that in my life.

I also never thought I could fall in love with a woman, but here I am, more in love with Olivia and Alex than I have ever been with anyone, including Andrew. And to think I thought that fucker was the love of my life... boy, was I wrong.

We get to the car, and I put a zombified Alex into the passenger seat and buckle him up.

"Are you even capable of functioning enough to go get our girl? Because if not, I am leaving your ass at home while I go get her!" I snapped at him. He doesn't deserve my attitude, but I'm annoyed and feeling particularly stabby.

Chapter Five

Olivia

I woke up the next morning in my bed with my stomach turning, a raging headache, and my eyes puffy from crying so much yesterday. I groan as I stretch and then try to rub the puffiness out of my eyes. Fuck I hate crying. When I sit up, my head starts to spin, causing my nausea to get worse. "Ughh," I grab my head, hoping my head will stop spinning long enough to get up and go pee.

I sling my legs over the side of the bed and try to stand, my knees giving out as soon as I put all my weight on them. I feel like a fucking hungover twenty-one-year-old who just got plastered for the first time. I sit back down on the bed and wait for a few minutes to let my head calm down. This is going to be a long day if I can't get my head to stop spinning.

I finally push off the bed to see if I can actually get on my feet and not fall over this time. My head starts to spin again, but I keep my balance. Finally, getting one foot in front of the other and slowly making my way to the bathroom, using the wall to hold me up.

I reach the bathroom, do my business, and then start washing my hands. When I look up from the flowing warm water and suds going down the drain, I catch sight of my reflection in the mirror. My eyes have bags under them, and I have bruises up and down my arms from being manhandled by Tony. I lift the hem of my shirt with trembling fingers, showing the canvas of red and purple bruises all over my body. Cuts criss-cross my skin like some fucking sadistic game of connect-the-dots. The game wasn't over until there wasn't anything left on my body untouched.

I then look down at my legs and see the bruises that match the rest of my body. How the fuck was anyone willing to bid on someone who was such a mess, someone with so many marks on them they looked like they were used for target practice? Are people really that desperate for a fuck toy? I can buy them a fucking sex robot if that's what they want.

I look back up at my face in the reflection, and I still see a hint of a handprint around my neck, from where Tony choked me until I passed out. That is when the first tear falls, and I have no energy to stop it. I let the floodgates open, and I cry. I cry for the person I was, I cry for the woman I am now, and most of all, I cry for the people I wasn't able to save.

But from this point forward, I will put my blood, sweat, and tears into saving every single person who is in human trafficking. I am going to take down Lopez

García and everyone involved with him. This shit is going to end now!

When I finally make it to the living room, I see Oliver lying there on the couch, awake, playing on his phone. I look at the kitchen for a cup of coffee, but decide against that. I need answers first.

"So, why the fuck are you here, Oliver? And don't lie to me. I'm tired of all the lies." I say with a no-bullshit tone as I collapse onto the couch next to him, throwing my arm over my face as if that could shield me from everything swirling inside my head.

Oliver takes a deep breath, as if this story is going to take everything out of him. Fucking dramatic as fuck. "Well, I guess we are cutting straight to the chase, are we?" He takes a deep breath like he is preparing for a whole speech.

"Dad told me about the call that Lopez García made when you were there. Dad was losing his shit, so I started digging, trying to figure out where you might be, where he would be holding you. After a while, I got a message from Alex on Facebook; he was also losing his mind over you being in the grasp of Lopez García. He went off the deep end, coming up with this insane plan about going to the auction and bidding on you, saying he'd win you, and I would be hiding, picking off the goons one by one, while he got you out of the way and back to safety."

"Oh really? He was there to save me? But he bid on me? That makes perfect fucking sense. He is just like his fucking grandfather. I swear to God I don't believe a damn word that comes out of his mouth." I am now sitting up, hands flaring through the air as I damn near scream at my brother because I am so furious.

Oliver's voice cracks with a mix of disbelief and frustration as he continues. "You have it wrong, Liv..."

He takes a deep breath, trying to calm himself. "He was seriously worried about you, and you know I wouldn't just say that shit. When I say Alex was ready to burn the whole fucking world down to get to you, I mean it. He was out of his mind. I don't think you actually realize how far he was willing to go just to get you back."

My brain is trying to process all that he is saying, but I don't want to believe it. I can barely grasp the weight of it all. My thoughts are a tangled mess, and the flood of information is starting to drown me.

"But López García told me that Alex wanted me..." I choke on the words, my throat tight with doubt and confusion. "He said Alex knew I was there, and he..."

Before I can finish, Oliver pulls me into a tight hug, his warmth grounding me during the storm raging in my head. My thoughts are swirling like a tornado that I can't escape. I can't help it, and I sob again, this time against his chest, this time the tears falling for the guilt of suspecting Alex and the heartbreaking truth that I don't know who to trust.

"Liv, I see you," Oliver whispers, his voice low and steady. "I can't even imagine what you went through, but you can't blame anyone besides the people who physically did this to you. Lopez García is to blame. Alex had nothing to do with it. I swear on my life. I can see it in the way he looks at you; he loves you more than anything, Liv. He loves you like crazy, or maybe he's just a little crazy, but please give him a chance to explain. If you still don't believe him, I will follow you out the door and make sure he never comes near you again." I just hug him tighter and sniffle into his chest.

Oliver knows me better than anyone. He can read my mind and knows how torn I am between what is true and what is a lie. I know he sees the battle raging inside me, the one I can't fight for myself.

"Fine. I will listen to what he has to say, but make no promises about anything."

"Deal." He whispers as he kisses my head and holds out his pinky to me. He knows that pinky promises are the most sacred form of promises. I wrap my pinky around his and kiss my thumb, sealing my fate.

Chapter Six

Alex

My phone starts buzzing in my pocket. I yank it out, and the moment I see the caller ID, my heart skips a beat.

Oliver.

I swipe to answer, trying to steady my voice.

"Hey, man, what's up? How's Olivia?" Concern flows into every word. I don't care about anything else right now; I just want to know she is safe.

"She's as good as she can be, considering what she has been through," Oliver replies, his voice heavy, which causes my stomach to drop.

"But I called to tell you I talked to her. She's willing to hear you out, but she was told some shit that was said to her while she was locked up. She thinks that you were involved in her kidnapping, that you and your grandfather set this whole thing up."

My chest tightens.

"It's gonna take a lot to convince her otherwise."

A heavy sigh escapes my mouth as the weight of it all crashes down on me. This is worse than I thought.

How the hell do I fix this?

What if she doesn't believe me when I tell her the truth? What if she thinks I'm just another liar, someone who got close to her just to sell her?

The outcome is a blur, and I don't know what waits for me on the other side of this conversation. But I do know one thing, this is for sure:

I owe it to her.
To Rachel.
And to myself.
To try.
To fix what I didn't know I broke.

To bring us all back together, no matter how impossible it feels.

"I'll do whatever it takes." The words tumble out before I can even think, but I don't take them back. "Thank you, Oliver. I owe you one." I say.

I will do anything to get Olivia back in my arms. The distance is unbearable. I need both of my women by my side to feel whole again.

"Alright, well, Olivia fell asleep on my lap after talking, so when she wakes up, I'll ask her when she wants to talk and let you know what she says. But... like I said, she's shaken up, and I can't promise anything."

Oliver ended the call before I could reply. The weight of this whole situation is crashing down on me. Now, I have to come up with a plan to win Olivia back. But first, I need to know what my grandfather told her. I would try to ask him, but I know that if I call him, he won't answer. The bastard's probably already ditched his phone and is hiding somewhere like the coward he is.

I glance up and spot Rachel striding toward me in her work suit, her red heels clicking sharply against the floor. Her red lipstick matched - bold, precise, and the same shade of crimson - her twisted up in some sleek, complicated style. I swear, I don't know the first damn thing about women's hairstyles, but whatever that is, it works. She looks so damn good. Confident and dangerous.

"Hey, big guy," Rachel says, looking up at me with a sexy smile on her face. "I need to go into the office, then I've got a meeting. Can you handle being home alone, or do you want to come with me? I've got a client I'm meeting with, but you're welcome to sit in if you'd like. Tyler will have to understand that the man owes me."

Tyler?

"You're meeting your client? Where? And why not at the office?" I bombard her with questions before she even has a chance to answer. What does this client want from her that can't be handled in the office?

"Tyler is Andrew's oldest brother. Yes, he's my client, and the business I'm helping him with can't be discussed in my office." Her response is vague, and I don't like it one bit. I don't know, Tyler, but I've seen how Andrew treated Rachel, and I refuse to let her go through that shit again.

"Cool. Let me change real quick, and I'll go with you. I don't trust this Tyler guy. If I'm being completely honest, I don't trust anyone affiliated with Andrew. So, I'll go with and make sure nothing stupid happens."

She raises an eyebrow, then grabs me by my shirt collar. "Aww, you're coming to keep me safe, big guy? The woman who killed more men last night than you did?" She pats my chest and laughs. "Alright, babe, whatever helps you sleep at night. But, I think my knives and I can handle ourselves just fine, thank you very much."

She turns and walks toward the garage, grabbing the keys off the hook as she passes. I follow right behind her, noticing she doesn't have the patience to wait for me to change out of my jeans and polo shirt.

"Rach, don't you want me to change into something more…" I look at her, confused. "Business-like?"

"Nope, you're fine. I just need to grab some papers from the office, real quick. You can stay in the car for that, and then we will go meet Tyler."

She gets into the 4Runner and starts it up. As I buckle into the passenger seat, I turn on the rock radio station I know she likes, and we head down the road to her office.

When we arrive at the office, Rachel parks in the front spot, jumps out of the car, and walks in. When she comes back, she gets back into the car, places a thick manila envelope on top of her bag in the back seat, buckles up, and starts heading back onto the highway.

My mind starts to wander about this meeting.

What's in that envelope?

"Alright, Muñeca, where's this meeting at?" I ask as she takes an exit I know all too well. My stomach drops with anticipation before she finally answers.

"The Silver Serpent."

"Fuck!" The words slip out before I can stop them. The one place in all of Southern California that she goes to is the Italians' casino. The Luciano family owns that place, and my grandfather's shitty relationship with them is the last thing I need repercussions for right now.

Maybe since I don't work for my grandfather, they'll be chill with me. Maybe they won't even recognize me. One can only hope for that outcome, but it's a long shot.

"My grandfather has made enemies with the Italians. The Silver Serpent's not the best place for a Lopez García to go." I glance at her, trying to get a read on her reaction.

When she turns her head for a second to look at me, her face pales. "I am so sorry; I didn't know, Alex." She grabs her phone to make a call. I snatch it from her before she can dial. "No. It's fine. We'll deal with the situation when it comes to us. They might not even recognize me since I don't work for my family. I don't personally have any problems with the Italians. Maybe it won't be a total shit show."

She looks skeptically at me. "Sorry, babe, but you do look like your grandfather. It's not hard to tell you belong to that bloodline."

"Well, fuck." I mutter under my breath as we pull up to the casino parking lot.

Chapter Seven

Rachel

I walk into the Silver Serpent, fingers laced with Alex's, the warmth of his hand grounding me. The casino hums with life—glasses clinking, soft jazz drifting through the air, slot machines spinning, and the occasional burst of cheers from a lucky winner. The scent of expensive whiskey and cigar smoke lingers in the air, mixing with the metallic tang of my own nerves.

Alex's muscles tighten beneath my touch as we move deeper inside. His grip on my hand hardens—not enough to hurt, but enough to tell me he's on edge.

"Hey, are you okay?" I ask, my voice low but full of concern.

"Yeah." His tone is clipped, his eyes scanning the room, sharp and calculating. "Just on high alert. I don't need a gunfight breaking out in the middle of this casino."

I stop mid-stride, pull his arm so he spins to face me, and glance up at him. "Wait—you're carrying a gun right now?"

He turns to me, eyes narrowing slightly. "Are you carrying knives on you?" He answers my question with a question. I give a sharp nod. "Exactly." His words were as sharp as the knives in question. "Ever since Olivia was taken, I've had a minimum of two on me at all times. I'm not taking any risks anymore." His voice is steady, but there's an edge to it. "Being a Lopez García is dangerous enough, but going against THE Lopez García? That's an even bigger risk. My grandfather will want my head for what happened at the auction, and I refuse to let you or Olivia be at risk again because of my family's bullshit."

I swallow hard and nod, unwilling to poke at that wound right now. This is neither the time nor the place for that conversation. I turn away from him, continuing to walk deeper into the casino as I scan every table and bar.

I finally spot Tyler Starr seated at a table in the far right corner of the bar. His messy red hair hangs in front of his face; his fingers are loosely curled around a glass of amber liquor, watching the liquid swirl, lost in thought.

"Come on," I say, tugging Alex toward the table. He follows, but I don't miss how his free hand hovers near his side, where I know one of his guns is hidden, and his hand laced in mine squeezes a little tighter, almost a sign to show me that he is here with me through it all.

"Tyler," I greet as we approach, keeping my voice even and professional. I always get a knot in my stomach from being near a Starr brother. After all the hell Andrew put me through, trusting them isn't an option.

Tyler looks up, giving us a practiced, unreadable smile. "Rachel. Thanks for meeting me here." He extends a hand. I hesitate for half a second before grabbing his hand to shake it, keeping my grip firm and professional. He looks over at Alex, then back at me. "And who is this?"

"This is my boyfriend, Alex," I say, my tone making it very clear where my loyalties lie.

Alex extends his hand out to Tyler, who takes it in his grip and shakes it, his gaze steadily watching Tyler's every move. Then, without a word, he pulls out a chair for me. It's a simple gesture, but one that speaks volumes—protection, possession, maybe even a warning.

I sit back straight, trying not to let my nerves show. Whatever Tyler wants, I need to be ready for it.

Tyler exhales sharply, swirling his drink again. "Rachel, the biggest reason I needed to talk to you so urgently is to let you know my brothers are pissed about what happened to Andrew." His eyes lift to meet mine, dark and brimming with unspoken rage. "He was murdered. We got all the reports back from the Medical Examiner; the cause of death was a stab wound to the throat."

I keep my features schooled, suppressing any flicker of emotion that could give me away.

Tyler leans in, resting his elbows on the table, staring me down like he's searching for a crack in my armor. "You have any idea who killed him?" His voice is lower now, edged with suspicion. "You were the last one to see him alive."

I mirror his posture, leaning forward with quiet confidence, even as my pulse pounds. Under the table, I feel Alex shift. His hand moves to his waistband.

"Don't you think if I knew who killed him, I would have told you?" I arch a brow, keeping my voice measured. "Are you accusing me of killing your brother, Tyler? If so, just spit it out instead of dancing around it."

Tyler leans back, crossing his arms over his chest, studying me.

"I'm not accusing shit, Rachel. Just stating facts."

"I already told you," I say evenly. "Andrew was involved in some deep shit. Someone probably killed him for crossing the wrong people or not paying a debt. I also have the report right here." I pull out the manila envelope I grabbed from the office. "It states he had Fentanyl and Heroin in his system before death."

Tyler's jaw tightens. His fingers flex against his biceps as if trying to restrain himself. Then, suddenly—

"YOU LIAR!" His voice erupts as he slams his fist against the table, the impact rattling the glasses. Heads turn. Conversations stop.

I flinch at the outburst—not because of fear, but because, for a split second, his voice sounds exactly like Andrew's.

"Excuse me? Would you like to have a look at the documents?" I say, forcing my tone to remain calm.

Tyler's nostrils flare. His hands tremble with barely contained fury. "We got the camera footage, Rachel." His voice is lower now, lethal. "You were the only one in and out of the apartment on the day of Andrew's death. You fucking killed him."

The air in the casino thickens. I barely register the murmurs around us before Tyler moves.

In one swift motion, he yanks out his gun and points it at my forehead.

Alex moves just as fast, with no hesitation. In the blink of an eye, he's on his feet, both of his guns drawn and locked on Tyler.

Silence.
A dangerous standoff.

The weight of the moment presses down on me. One wrong move, one twitch of a finger, and blood will spill all over the velvet carpet, and it will be my fault.

I steady my breathing, my pulse hammering in my ears.

This has just gotten a hell of a lot more complicated.

Chapter Eight

Olivia

I wake up from my nap, finally feeling more human. It's been days since I have felt decent. I blink to adjust my eyes to the soft glow of the TV and glance over to see Oliver sprawled on the couch, eyes locked on an action movie.

"Hey, sorry I fell asleep," I mumble, my voice still thick with sleep.

Oliver glances over, a slight smirk tugging at his lips. "Don't be sorry, sissy. You needed it. And as I told you, I'm here with you every step of the way."

Before I can respond, his phone buzzes loudly on the coffee table. Oliver glances at the screen, and just for a second, something flickers across his face—hesitation, maybe even dread. Then he snatches it up, pressing it to his ear, and his body stiffens.

"Alex. What's up?" Oliver's voice booms through my tiny apartment, followed by a long pause. Too long. My stomach tightens, my anxiety creeping in like a slow poison, taking over my body.

"Yeah, I'll be there..." Oliver's voice is steady, but I don't miss the flicker of concern in his blue-green eyes that match mine. Another silence stretches between him and Alex.

"She won't just stay here. You know that," he says, his tone firm. "Regardless of how confused she is with everything that happened, she won't do that."

What in the actual fuck are they talking about?

"Yeah. Okay. Mhm. Bye."

Oliver hangs up, but before he can even lower his phone, I'm already glaring daggers at him.

"What the fuck is going on?" I demand my pulse, now a thunderous roar in my ears.

Oliver lifts his hands in surrender. "Okay. So before you freak out—"

"Before I freak out? That's the worst fucking thing to say to someone before they freak out! Are you serious right now? Just spit it out, Oli!" I snap, my patience gone.

He exhaled, rubbing the back of his neck. "Alex and Rachel are outside the Silver Serpent. Andrew's oldest brother, Tyler, accused Rachel of killing Andrew and pulled a gun on her. Alex and Rachel barely got away, but they knew the Starr brothers would be coming after them. And we don't know who they're bringing with them."

I clench my fists, my mind racing.

"Alex asked if I knew anyone in San Diego who could help with this situation. Lopez García and Alex aren't on good terms, so his family isn't gonna back him up."

That stops me cold in my tracks.

If Lopez García isn't helping Alex, then they aren't aligned with him. So Alex wasn't involved in my capture.

My breath catches. A part of me wants to believe it—desperately. But another part, the one still raw and bleeding from the inside out, refuses to let go of the doubt. Then why did he buy me? Why did he make it so dramatic? Why didn't he come for me sooner if he knew where I was the whole time? Was Rachel in on it as well?

I shove those thoughts aside. Answers can wait. Right now, Alex and Rachel need me, and I will be damned if another Starr brother hurts Rachel.

"Well, then let's go get them," I say, determination hardening my voice. "You make the calls and get Dad to work his sources. I'll get out of these pajamas and strap up."

I don't wait for his response when I turn on my heels and sprint to my closet, yanking off my pajamas as I go.

I mentally go through my checklist as I get dressed.

Dark, form-fitting jeans—on.

Black shirt—on.

Tactical harness—strapped tight.

Two guns—holstered- loaded.

Leather jacket—slid over my shoulders.

Two more guns— holstered on the inside of my

jeans—loaded.

Boots—secured.

Knives—slid inside their sheaths and strapped in.

I glance at myself in the mirror, my chest rising and falling with adrenaline. My fingers curl into fists.

No one threatens what's mine, and I will make sure the whole world knows that!

Oliver and I pull up to the Silver Serpent. The parking lot is packed, forcing us to drive past it to the empty dirt lot in the back. Gravel crunches under the tires as Oliver parks and kills the engine of my Cadillac.

"Call Alex. Let him know where we are," I say, scanning the area. "And where the hell are Dad's guys?"

Oliver gives me a pointed look. "They're my guys, too, Liv. I am Dad's underboss."

I freeze.

The words hit me harder than I expected, cutting through my focus like a blade.

I am Dad's underboss.

This is the first time Oliver has admitted—flat-out—that he and Dad have been living the mafia life without me, keeping me out and excluding me from it.

My chest tightens, stinging more than I'd like to admit. But I shove it down. Rachel and Alex need me right now; I don't have time to think about my feelings.

I force a nod, swallowing the lump in my throat. "Fine. Just tell me they're coming."

"They're coming. Calm down, Liv."

Just hearing those words makes something in me snap.

I let out a short, humorless laugh. "Calm down?"

Then the dam breaks, and I let it flow.

"CALM DOWN?" My voice erupts, raw and unfiltered, shaking the air between us.

"I was physically held captive and raped by the biggest drug lord in Southern fucking California and his right-hand man! Then they put me up for auction like I was cattle! I fucking lost the two loves of my fucking life! All because I don't know who's telling me the damn truth and who's not! And now? Now I find out you and Dad have been lying to me my entire fucking life about our family being the MAFIA! And on top of all of that, dumbass, Andrew's brothers are gunning for two of the most important people in my life. So please, Oliver, please tell me to 'calm the fuck down' again! Because I have every right to be pissed! Every fucking right not to be calm!"

I'm screaming, arms flailing, my entire body trembling with rage and exhaustion.

Oliver's face drains of color. He looks like I just gutted him. And maybe, with my words, I did. He knows he fucked up.

"I'm sorry, Liv." His voice is quieter now, softer. "That's not what I meant. You have every reason to be angry, not to be calm. I just meant... trust me. I won't let this fall apart. I swear to you."

I flinch at his words, 'trust me.' The one statement I don't know how to handle yet. His apology is genuine. I can hear it. Feel it.

But right now, my brain is everywhere, and I don't know if I can trust anyone.

I sit in the Cadillac, gripping the edge of the seat so hard my knuckles ache. The glow of the casino lights flickers across the windshield, but I don't see them. My mind is a storm, the kind that drowns reason and leaves nothing but raw, seething rage.

I know Rachel and Alex are watching me through the window. I can feel the weight of their stares, the tension stretching tight between us. I don't look at them. If I do, I'll break, and I can't afford that. Not now. Not when everything inside me is still screaming.

Gravel crunches. Engines hum low, almost a growl, as four blacked-out Chevrolet Suburbans roll in beside us. My pulse, already frayed, tightens like a wire.

"Are these your guys?" I don't take my eyes off the vehicles as I glance at Oliver.

He gives a slight nod.

Fucking great. Here goes nothing.

Chapter Nine

Alex

I glance over at the Cadillac, my stomach tightening when I see Olivia sitting there, her blue-green eyes burning with fury as she glares at the casino. I don't know what's going through her beautifully dangerous mind, but one thing is clear—she's pissed, the kind of pissed that leads to bad decisions.

"You gonna stare at her all night, or are you gonna grow a pair and fix this?" Rachel says, irritation dripping from her words as she sits in the driver's seat, fingers tapping impatiently on the steering wheel. She's barely holding it together, just like me. We both want our girl back, but apparently, this is only my fault, thanks to my fucking grandfather.

"Yes, Rachel, I'll fix it!" I snap, dragging a hand through my hair. I want to be mad at her, but I know why she's angry, and I know that I'm the only one who can fix this. I take a deep breath before anything, trying to calm my words; she doesn't deserve my harsh words.

"I just don't know how to yet." I steal another glance at Olivia through the tinted windows, the weight of unspoken words pressing down on me like a thousand-pound brick...

I have to switch this conversation before my guilt eats me alive, and I am no use to them with this Starr brothers situation. "Any word on the Starr brothers? Have they left the casino?" I ask. "No, they should all still be in there." Rachel's voice tightens, her frustration bubbling over. "And now it all makes sense. Andrew was deep in with the Italians, always at the casino, drinking and gambling. Hell, he was in so much debt they showed up at our damn apartment demanding payment more times than I can count." Her face twists with anger, and she clenches the steering wheel so tight her knuckles start turning white.

I place a hand on her shoulder, trying to ground her. "Rach, Andrew's dead. No one's coming after you. And if they try, I will make them regret every choice they have made in life, especially going for my girls." My voice is steel, final, and unwavering. My hand moves up to her face, cupping her cheek. "No one will take what's mine ever again."

I feel Rachel move out of my grip. "Looks like Oliver's guys are here. I guess it's time to get out and face the music," she groans, pushing the door open to step out of the car.

We both get out and walk in front of the 4Runner. Oliver and Olivia join us, and then I see Oliver nod his head at the four Chevrolet Suburbans. The men file out and come to stand in a semicircle around us.

Oliver clears his throat. "So, what's the plan, Alex? Where are the Starr brothers? Are they all involved with the Italians fully or just in debt to them because of Andrew?" Alright, I guess we're getting straight to the point. But it's not me who replies. "As far as we know, the Starr brothers are still in there. I am not sure they are fully involved. We need to get more info before we figure out what to do next." Rachel lays it all out for them. I turn my head and see Olivia watching her every move, longing, and sorrow in her eyes.

"Ok, well, since they don't know me, I will walk in and scope out the area, you two," Oliver points with split fingers at Rachel and me. "They know, so it's a liability for you to go in. We need to determine where we need to go, who is involved, and how to target only the Starr brothers. We don't want further problems with the Italians if we can avoid it." Oliver is entirely at ease, putting plans into action and assigning tasks to his team.

Olivia stands by her brother, arms crossed, a scowl on her face. They look so much alike when they stand by each other; the only difference right now is that you can see Oliver is in full boss-man mode, and Olivia is ready to murder anyone who looks at any of us the wrong way. I have never seen this level of anger from her before, and it's both terrifying and incredibly sexy.

Before I even realize what I'm doing, I walk up to Olivia and hold out my hand, silently pleading that she take it and let me explain, but she doesn't. Instead, she steps back just a fraction. She doesn't say a word. Not even a glare. Just that fraction of a space that suddenly feels like I'm miles away from her again. My stomach caves in like she knocked the wind out of me. One singular step. Not even a full one. Just a twitch of her heel was enough to make my whole world tilt.

She looks at me like I'm another problem she has to deal with, another weight pressing down on her already burdened shoulders. To my right, I see Rachel step around me, offering her hand, and Olivia takes it without hesitation. No second-guessing.

It feels worse than a punch to the gut. I want to be happy that she trusts one of us, but I'm not; I feel every other negative emotion imaginable. I'm furious with my grandfather, pissed at myself, frustrated with everything, and most of all, desperate. Just fucking desperate.

I tell myself I shouldn't be surprised. Olivia's been keeping me at arm's length ever since the night at the auction. Since she started questioning whether I was just another man trying to take advantage of her, or if I was still her Alex. But knowing why she's pulling away doesn't make it any easier to handle.

My fingers curl into a fist at my side as I force myself to breathe through it. This isn't about me. It never was.

But damn, it still cuts deep.

Rachel glances at me, something unreadable flickering in her eyes like she knows exactly how much that moment wrecked me. Maybe she does. She's always been better at understanding Olivia than I am.

I shift my weight, trying to shake the feeling creeping into my chest. Now isn't the time to dwell on this. We have a job to do. People to deal with. The Starr brothers, the Italians—everything else is more important than my wounded pride.

But as Oliver continues forming the plan, my eyes keep finding Olivia, drawn to the way her jaw tightens, her fingers twitching at her side like she's barely holding herself back. She's still furious, still walking that razor-thin line between control and chaos.

And I should be worried about what happens when she finally snaps.

But all I can think about is whether she'll ever reach for me again.

And God, I don't know what will destroy me first... Her rage, or her silence.

Chapter Ten

Olivia

I don't know what I hate more—the situation, the men inside that casino, or the fact that a part of me still wants to trust Alex even after everything that happened to me.

But trust got me into this situation in the first place, so trust is not very easy for me right now.

Oliver starts to speak, his voice commanding as he lays out the next part of the plan. He's always been the one to take control of the situations we have been in. To think instead of acting on impulse. Right now, I wish I had that ability. Instead, my pulse pounds with rage, my fingers twitching at my sides, aching to do something, anything, to feel like I have control again.

And then Alex steps toward me, hand outstretched.

My eyes stare at his hand, and my breath catches. For a split second, my body betrays me, and muscle memory draws me toward his familiarity, the way his fingers used to anchor me, the way he once made the world feel a little less dangerous. My fingers almost move toward his.

Almost.

But then the moment shatters, my mind going back to the auction, and I take a hesitant step back.

His face doesn't change much, but I see it— the flicker of hurt in his eyes and the slight tensing of his jaw. The ghosts of all the unspoken words linger between us. I should feel victorious for keeping him at a distance, for proving to myself that I don't need him, but all I feel is something hollow and aching in my chest, the missing piece of my heart. Why can't my mind make up what it wants to do? Why is this situation so difficult? Oliver was right when he said that Alex is not his grandfather, but why can't I get past it? Why is there still an ache in my chest?

Then, I notice movement next to Alex, and Rachel steps forward, offering her hand to me. I grab it. No hesitation. No uncertainty. I take it without even thinking twice.

As soon as I have her hand in mine, I feel secure. She's steady. Familiar. Safe. She's been with me through the worst of it, and right now, I need something solid to hold on to. Something that won't slip through my fingers like everything else has these past few months. Every good thing that has happened seems to be falling apart, and she is holding my jagged pieces for me.

When my fingers close around hers, I feel Alex break behind me. It's not just something I imagine. I hear his breath falter, feel the shift in the air, the weight of his presence retreating.

A part of me screams to turn around, to see if he's still standing there, to see if I've finally cut the last tether between us.

But I don't.

If I do, I might lose the last shred of resolve I have left. I can't let him back in. I can't risk it.

Not when I still don't know if he's the one I need to escape from.

Not when I still don't know if I'd even want to.

Oliver's words repeat in my mind, but the what-ifs won't let me go.

Chapter Eleven

Rachel

Olivia's hand in mine makes my heart feel like it's finally back where it belongs. The chaos around us fades for just a moment, and all that matters is that she's here, safe by my side. I didn't realize how much I missed her and needed her presence until now, when I felt her grounding me in all this. She's always been the missing piece I didn't know I needed.

Unfortunately, the calm doesn't last long.

Oliver's voice cuts through the thick, heavy air. Sharp and focused. He's laying out the plan, his tone steady, controlled. It's what he does best: taking charge and strategizing .

I feel Olivia tense beside me with every word he says, her fingers tightening around mine like I am her lifeline.

"I will go in, check out the place, and act like a customer. I'll have an earpiece in so everyone can hear what I'm saying. I'll give a play-by-play of what I see as well."

I feel her pulse pounding against my palm. I know her mind is already racing ahead, trying to anticipate every worst-case scenario. She's not just anxious; she's *terrified*. That's her twin walking into a bad situation.

"I'll go with you!" The words burst from Olivia's mouth like she couldn't hold them in any longer. Her voice is sharp, desperate, vibrating with the kind of urgency that makes the entire group fall silent. Every head turns to her. The fire in her eyes burns hot, daring anyone to challenge her.

And, of course, Alex does.

"Like hell, you will!" His voice slices through the quiet like a blade. His demand is loud and confident. I don't even have to look at him to know that anger, frustration, and, most of all, fear are written all over his face. He thinks he hides his emotions well, but I can read him like a book.

"We just got you back," he says, his voice edged with something raw. "I'm not going to lose you again."

The air around us suddenly feels suffocating under the weight of his words. I know he means well; he's trying to protect her, but if he pushes her too hard... I don't want it to come to that.

Olivia's head snapped in Alex's direction. "Well, I didn't know you had any say in what I fucking do, Alex." Her voice cracked like a whip, leaving no room for argument.

I feel her let go of my hand, and the absence of her touch is a sudden, jarring cold that seeps into my bones. She crosses her arms, her chin lifting in defiance, star-

ing Alex down like he's just another obstacle she's prepared to bulldoze through.

*A fiery redhead with a spine made of steel. A girl who
never backs down from a fight, especially when it comes
to her damn freedom that she just got back.*

Alex doesn't move. His jaw clenches so tightly that I
swear I can hear his teeth grinding, but his *eyes* betray
him; there is a flicker of vulnerability beneath the fury.
The fear of losing her again is visible to the world, just
for a second, before you see him bury it.

His voice softens, but the tension remains ra-
zor-sharp. "I didn't mean it like that, Olivia." There's
a hesitation now, a slight crack in his armor. "I'm not
trying to tell you what to do. I just don't want to lose you
again. If anything happens..."

His voice trails off. Watching this is breaking my
heart for both of them.

And Olivia, she doesn't miss a beat.

She steps closer, and her following words hit harder
than any scream ever could.

"But you want me to let my fucking twin go into the
unknown by himself? Risk his life for all of us, by himself?"

Silence.

Thick. Heavy. Suffocating. Silence...

Alex has no answer, and Olivia knows it. Her words
hang between them, slicing through whatever argument
he might have had. She's not asking for permission.

She's not asking for protection. She's demanding equality. If Oliver can take the risk, so can she.

The weight of it all presses down on me. On *us*. The room holds its breath, waiting for someone to break the tension.

Alex swallows, but he doesn't reply. Olivia doesn't need one; she will do this regardless of who says no.

While they are both at a standstill, I'm just standing in the middle of the storm, watching the collision of two people who are too stubborn, broken, and *afraid* to meet each other halfway. And somehow, I know this fight isn't even close to being over.

Olivia turns around and walks away from the group, ending the conversation where it stood.

Chapter Twelve

Alex

I can't let her walk away again. I can't lose her again. I may have pissed her off, but she is mine, no matter what. Regardless of the chaos that is going on, I refuse to let this woman go.

Before I can stop myself, I grab her arm and pull her into me. Wrapping my arms around her waist, desperate to fuse her to me, to make sure she knows exactly where she belongs. With me. With us.

She sucks in a sharp breath, her body tense against mine. I reach up, tilting her chin so she has no choice but to look at me. Her beautiful blue-green eyes blaze with a challenge—a silent dare.

I do the only thing I can think of and bend down to kiss her. Not just a soft and gentle kiss but a hard, demanding, and owning kiss. I pour everything into that kiss: every ounce of frustration, devotion, and love. Claiming her the only way I know how. Silently begging her to understand that I had nothing to do with her capture and to trust me.

For a second, she doesn't move.

For a second, I think I've lost her for good.

But then I feel her walls shatter. A small noise escapes her, barely a gasp, and she kisses me back. Her hands fly up, gripping the hair on the back of my neck, pulling me in closer, like she needs this just as much as I do.

My heart skips a beat, and I know I'm finally home.

When she pulls away, her breath is ragged, her lips swollen, and tears are streaming down her face. "Pl-please tell me my mind is lying to me." Her voice is barely a whisper, but the weight of those words nearly breaks me.

Another tear slips down her cheek, and I reach up, wiping it away with my thumb. "I promise you, Azúcar," I murmur, voice thick. "I had nothing to do with my grandfather's evil. I would never, EVER let him take you. You are the love of my life, and I would never want to hurt you." I cup her face, forcing her to hear every word. "You and Rachel complete my broken black soul. I would never willingly jeopardize that."

She doesn't answer right away. Instead, she turns, looking at Oliver. Their silent conversation is immediate, a twin connection I'll never fully understand. And then, Oliver nods. Whatever Olivia sees in his face is enough.

She turns back to me, lips parting slightly, and I see it for the first time in what feels like forever.

Hope.

"I love you, Alex." Her voice is still hesitant, still broken, but I hold my breath because she's not running.

"This is going to take time to grow again," she warns. "I am fucked up, broken, and damaged, but I am willing to give us a chance." Her gaze flickers to Rachel. "The three of us."

She reaches out for Rachel, and without a second thought, Rachel grabs Olivia's hand, fingers threading together with ease. Olivia pulls her close, and the moment Olivia is completely in our embrace, I feel the tension in her shoulders release just slightly.

It's a small surrender, a step forward. But it is a small victory I will gladly accept.

Rachel presses a soft kiss to the back of Olivia's head, then leans in, her voice soft, warm, and undeniable. "Always remember, babe." Another kiss, a little firmer. "He is ours. You belong to me, and I to you. We belong together."

A pulse of electricity shoots through me at Rachel's words, lighting up every part of me.

I have never known love the way I feel it now.
Not in my heart.
Not in my soul.
Not in my whole damn body.

Chapter Thirteen

Olivia

"I love you, Alex. I really do, but that doesn't change the fact that I'm going in with Oliver." My voice is steady, but my heart pounds like a war drum. "I have to be his backup; we are twins; it's what we do. The Italians and the Starr brothers don't know us; we will be in and out before you know it. We'll have earpieces also; you'll hear every move we make throughout the casino."

I search his face for understanding, trust, or maybe even permission. My heart and gut are at war, but I have to believe him. I have to trust that he's on my side, at least right now. I do.

I want him. I want him more than anything. Rachel and Alex are my home, and deep down, I know that has never changed and never will.

Alex exhales sharply, his jaw clenching like he's physically biting back his protest. "I don't like this, but I hear you. Just..." He shakes his head, frustration and fear tangled in his expression. "I'm scared to lose you. So you better not die." His laugh is nervous and humorless.

I force a small smirk, though my stomach twists. "I wouldn't dream of it." I get up on my tippy toes and give him a quick peck on the lips. But deep down, I know that's a promise I might not be able to keep.

I step back from him, peeling my body away from the warmth of his arms, the safety I desperately want to sink into. But I can't. Not yet. I turn toward Oliver, rolling my shoulders as adrenaline starts to pump through me. "Alright, boss man. Let's get this shit done."

Finally, I'm not just surviving; I'm doing something. Something for my family. Both of them.

Oliver and I move through the grand entrance of the Silver Serpent as we belong here, our invisible earpieces linking us to Alex, Rachel, and the rest of Oliver's team.

The casino hums with life - laughter, the clink of glasses, and the distant chime of a jackpot, followed by a cheer. The air is thick with cigarette smoke and the scent of expensive cologne. We drift through the tables, pausing just enough to look natural, watching, listening, and occasionally cheering on someone who just won.

And then, I see him. Sitting at a crescent-moon-shaped table in the bar, a man with sharp features and rigid posture, it's like looking at Andrew, just older. However, it's not; he's dead, according to Alex and Rachel.

Five men surround him. Italians. Chatting, laughing, drinking, acting as if they didn't just threaten Rachel... My Rachel...

"Oliver. Slightly to your left, a crescent-moon table. A guy with shaggy red hair, wearing a black suit, surrounded by Italians."

Oliver doesn't react immediately, but I feel the shift in his energy. A barely visible glance, his jaw tightening.

"One of the Starr brothers?" He whispered to me.

"Has to be. Looks just like Andrew, just cleaner and older."

"Which one?"

I shake my head. "I don't know, but does it matter?"

We walk over to a nearby table, pretending to play, as every sense is honed in on them. The way they lean in close, the way their voices drop when they talk.

Then, I hear a name that catches my attention.

They're talking about Andrew. About his debt.

And then, Rachel's name. "...use her as payment." My blood turns to ice.

I grip the edge of the table, forcing my breath to stay calm, even though all I want to do is rip their fucking throats out. They want to trade my girl like she's property. Like she's nothing.

A predator's rage awakens in me, dark and deadly. The memories of when I was held against my will and sold like property are at the forefront of my memory, causing the rage to deepen. My fists tighten under the table, nails digging into my palms until the pain grounds me. I can't react, not yet.

But they will pay for this.

I swallow the fire in my throat and force my voice to stay steady. "Oliver. I can't lose her."

Oliver's gaze flicks to me; I know he heard the fear in my voice. "You won't. We're just here for intel, nothing more. We don't act on anything until we have a solid plan."

I nod. Force me to focus. To listen.

Three more Starr brothers walk into the bar, followed by an Italian man.

Dark brown, almost black hair. Deep, piercing brown eyes that could kill with a look. Stubble lines his jaw, giving him an edge of ruggedness and confidence to top it off.

As soon as the Italian man enters, the air in the casino shifts. It's not just me who notices. Oliver goes still beside me, his entire posture changing, his usual confidence replaced by something I can't quite place.

Recognition? Fear?

I hear him suck in a sharp breath, almost inaudible, and my gut twists. I turn to look at him, my voice low. "Oliver."

He doesn't respond. His eyes are locked on the Italian, his expression unreadable. I glance between them a couple of times. The man walks with power, with the kind of quiet dominance that demands respect. He's no ordinary associate. He's someone important.

And Oliver...He knows him. I know he does. His fingers twitch at his side, his jaw tightens, and when he finally exhales, it's slow. Measured.

Why is he acting like this?

"Oliver." I try again, but a little sharper this time.

Finally, his eyes flick to mine, but there's something in them I don't like. A hesitation. A shadow.

And for the first time in my life, I don't know what my twin is thinking. He's hiding something. That realization slams into me like a punch to the gut.

And I don't have time to unpack it. Oliver tears his gaze away and mutters, "Let's leave." His tone is final. No discussion. No explanation.

I swallow hard.

He's my brother. My twin. I trust him, but do I really know everything about him? A question I don't get to ask. Because right now, we have bigger problems. And whatever Oliver is hiding from me will have to wait.

I nod. It's game time.

They want to threaten my woman? They have no fucking idea what I'm capable of.

No one has seen the crazy in me come out, but the Starr brothers are about to get an up-close-and-personal look at her.

Chapter Fourteen

Rachel

We are sitting in the 4Runner; the speaker is cranked up loud so we don't miss a single word that Oliver or Olivia says.

"...use her as payment," I hear Samuel say; I think it's him. I've only met the other Starr brothers once, and their voices blur together in my memory. If I were looking at them, I'd know for sure, but right now, all I have is their cold, detached words.

"Oliver. I can't lose her." My breath caught in my throat at the raw desperation in Olivia's voice. It's almost a whisper, a plea, something fragile breaking beneath all her fire.

"You won't. We're just here for intel, nothing more. We don't act on anything until we have a solid plan." Oliver's commanding voice takes over, firm and rational.

When I glance at Alex, I see his jaw clenched and his expression dark. He doesn't like sitting back and just listening. "They won't get me. I promise." I grab Alex by the face, turn him towards me, and kiss him quickly, grounding him and myself for just a second before turning my attention back to the speaker.

So, the Starr brothers want me. That much is clear. And if it gets them to crawl out from whatever dark hole they slithered into, I'd gladly be bait. I'd walk right into the fire as long as my family doesn't burn with me.

"Let's leave." Oliver's voice cuts through my thoughts, interrupting my vengeful plans before I can even fully form them.

I need Olivia. Right now!

Before I even realize I'm moving, I throw the door open and bolt from the 4Runner, my pulse hammering in my ears. I need to see her, hold her, let her know I'm okay, and make sure she doesn't do something reckless. I know her, and I know what's brewing inside her beautiful head right now, the same thing boiling inside me.

RAGE!

When I reach Olivia, I see it—the pure, seething hatred in her eyes.

My stomach clenches. She's not just mad; she's beyond that. This is a storm, a hurricane of wrath swirling inside her, and I don't know if anyone can stop it.

When she reaches me, she doesn't say a word, just wraps me in her arms, crushing me against her chest. I bury my face into her chest, breathing her in, smelling her floral scent that I have missed so much, and feeling her rapid breathing. I can tell she's barely holding herself together.

"They won't get you, Rachel. The Starr brothers will die before any of them lays a finger on you," her voice strained and determined.

I know she means it. She'd burn the whole fucking world down for me without a second thought. That should terrify me, but all it does is make me love her even more.

I tilt my head up, searching her face, and for just a second, I see the rage in her eyes soften. Love and something darker flicker in her eyes, like obsession, or maybe possession?

"I know, babe. I know you won't let anything happen to me." I press a soft kiss to her lips, a silent promise just between us.

"I love you." And even as I say it, I wonder if love is what's keeping Olivia tethered to me, or is it the very thing pushing her closer to the edge?

Olivia cups my cheek, her thumb brushing over my skin with a tenderness that contradicts the storm raging in her eyes. Then she pulls me in, her lips crashing against mine in a kiss far more demanding than my own.

Her hands find my waist, gripping me tight, pulling me flush against her as she deepens the kiss even further. Heat floods through me as my body molds to hers. Her tongue glides along the seam of my lips, asking for entrance that I give eagerly. Our tongues collide in a battle for dominance, both unwilling to yield completely and desperate to claim the other.

She tastes like adrenaline and fire, like something untamed and all-consuming. Something that feels like home and yet scares me in the best way.

I don't want to lose her. Not again.

A throat clears behind us, yanking us back to reality.

"Alright, you two. We have a plan to form. You can suck each other's faces off later."

Oliver's voice carries a teasing edge, and I feel the heat rise to my cheeks. Olivia doesn't even flinch; instead, she throws a middle finger over her shoulder without breaking contact with my lips.

Then, with one more press of her lips to mine, she finally pulls away but keeps her hand on my hip, pulling me close so there's no gap between us.

We get back to Alex's house, and everyone piles into the office. Olivia sits on the couch, pulling me onto her lap, not letting there be any space between us.

"So, what's the plan?" Alex is staring directly at Oliver, who seems distracted as he stares at the desk. I wonder what happened in the casino that caused his whole demeanor to shift. I turn and look at Olivia, raising my eyebrow at her. I know she can also see the shift. She shakes her head and pulls me tighter, burying her face in my back, making sure I don't get off her lap.

"We need to figure out what ties the Starr brothers have to the Italians," Oliver says without looking up from the desk.

I look back at Olivia, who is staring at Oliver with wonder. Without breaking her stare, she speaks up next. "We need to make sure they get nowhere near Rachel and end it before it even begins."

Olivia grabs me and sets me down next to her before she stands and heads straight for Oliver, who still looks lost in thought.

"Oli," She says to him, causing him to lift his gaze just enough to look at her, nod, and follow her out of the office.

I watch them until the door shuts, and I turn to look at Alex leaning against the wall; his leg is bent against the wall, and his arms are crossed. His frustration was apparent on his face.

"You good?" I look at Alex, eyebrow raised in question.

"Hmm? Oh yeah, I'm fine." He looks at me. He must have been lost in thought also.

Chapter Fifteen

Olivia

We walk out into the hallway, and Oliver turns to me. He looks at me, but his eyes look so dead.

"Want to tell me what has you distracted? You haven't been yourself since we left the casino."

He shakes his head in response. God, this man is going to make me mad if he doesn't spit it out real soon.

"Oliver, I am not stupid. What is going on? Why do you look like you have seen the ghost of your past?"

He looks down at me in shock, like I just hit the nail on the head.

"Ah. The ghost of your past. Got it. Please just tell me if it was a Starr brother or the Italian." I cross my arms in front of my chest. Waiting for Oliver to spit it out. I don't need him to have a past with the Starr brothers, where he tries to stop me from ripping them apart piece by piece.

"Ugh. Why do you have to push Liv? I don't want to talk about it."

"Fine! Don't talk about it. But stop sulking so we can get this plan sorted out, and my girl isn't still stuck in the fucking crossfire!" I shoulder-check him as I walk back toward the office, and he grabs me by my wrist.

"Fine! I'll tell you, Liv. Just give me a second to get my words together." He lets out a dramatic sigh.

"Alessio.. That is his name." I raise an eyebrow at him to get him to continue talking.

"We have met before. When Dad and I went to Italy when we were sixteen, to handle some *business*, he was there. He is the son of Antonio Luciano." He stops to look at me again; this time, I see a whirlwind of emotions raging in his eyes.

"Who is Antonio Luciano?" I ask. I think he keeps forgetting that I don't know anything about the mafia world he has lived in.

"Antonio Luciano runs the biggest mafia family in Italy. We went over there because of an issue with the New York Luciano side. It turned out to be just a mix-up. We made a deal, and now we're on the same side."

I am listening to everything he says, but my brain can only focus on the part where he is talking to me, as if I have been involved with all of this the whole time. As if he and Dad didn't exclude me for almost thirty-five fucking years. My heart squeezes with betrayal. I don't want to have resentment against my family, but here it is, showing its ugly face..

"Alright, so you went to Italy to lay down your law and met Alessio. Why are you acting like you have seen a fucking ghost?"

He looks frustrated. "I am getting there, you impatient fuck!" He spits out.

I grab him by his chin and pull his head down to look at me. He has a good six inches on me, but I still have the bigger balls between the two of us.

"I don't know who the fuck died and made you king, but you better watch your fucking tone with me. We may be twins, but I will still take your ass down. You know we don't do that!" I look at him with daggers, making sure he knows how serious I am.

He jerks his chin out of my grip and turns away from me. "We had a thing." He turns back towards me. Pissed off and ready to fight someone. "Happy now?"

I cross my arms. "Actually? No, I am not happy. You are treating me as if I were some stupid little girl who needs protection. I haven't been involved in OUR family's business ever. You and Dad have shielded me, as if I were incompetent. Now you are half-ass telling me the truth about a guy I can tell you care for, or fucking fear!" I throw my hands up in the air in surrender. "So I guess this is how this is going to go! We are just going to lie to each other and half-ass tell me stuff. Cool, thanks for that. So much for keeping stuff from each other."

I turn around and walk away before Oliver can stop me, marching back into the office. I am fucking fuming and need to get rid of this rage. I walk over to the couch, grab Rachel's hand, pulling her up, and then walk to Alex and grab his hand. I drag them out of the office. Everyone in the office watches us as we leave with their jaws on the floor.

I pull them up the stairs towards the master bedroom, slamming the door open as I drag them along. When we are all through, I kick the door shut, let go of their hands, and turn to face them.

"Strip! Now! Both of you!" I command.

Chapter Sixteen

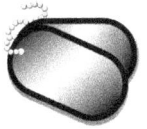

Alex

Olivia storms back into the office, pissed off at the world. When she grabs Rachel's hand, a pain of jealousy runs through me. Then she turns to me, grabs my hand, and storms right back out of the office—a woman on a mission. Everyone saw the shock on my face as I was dragged along.

I don't know what happened between Oliver and Olivia, but if this is the outcome I get, I will not complain one bit.

She practically drags us up the stairs to the master bedroom before slamming the door shut behind us.

She lets go of our hands, walks a few steps in front of us, and says, "Strip! Now! Both of you!" Her voice is sharp and powerful as she turns around towards us, looking directly at me.

"On your knees," she commands.

I instantly dropped to my knees without a single hesitation. My knees hit the floor with an audible thud, but

I don't feel the pain. I have never been submissive to a woman. But these two women could get me to beg like a dog for just a drop of affection.

Movement to my left catches my attention, and Rachel starts to drop to the floor next to me. Olivia's voice rings out through the room, stopping Rachel mid-squat. "Not you, Rachel," and she crooks her finger in a come-hither motion. "You are going to stand up here with me."

Rachel stands back up and walks up to her. I watch every move she makes, every sway of her hip, looking like a goddess. Every curve of her body is on display, and I am soaking in every minute of it.

My eyebrow arches as my eyes move to Olivia. "Are you going to strip, too, or do you get to be the only one with the view?"

A wicked smile spreads on her face as she bends down and grabs my chin, lifting it so my eyes meet hers. "Listen here, brat! I am making the rules here tonight. So, you just sit there and look pretty while I play with my food for a little bit." She pats my cheek before she stands back up and walks over to Rachel.

Holy fucking hell, that was sexy as fuck!

I look over at my girls as soon as Olivia gets back to Rachel, picking her up from behind her knees, and walks her to the bed, tossing her onto it. Rachel goes flying through the air and lands perfectly in the center with a fit of squeals and giggles.

The show in front of my eyes is better than anything I have ever seen. My eyes go back to Olivia, who is sashaying towards Rachel while slowly and torturously stripping out of her jeans, pushing down one side with her thumbs, and then moving to the other side.

Let the show begin.

I untuck my legs from under me and lean against the wall, my cock painfully hard. I wrap my hand around it, getting myself ready to enjoy my perfect view of my perfect girls.

As if she senses it, Olivia turns around to look at me and shakes her head, tsking at me. "You are on a real brat streak tonight, aren't you?" She looks down at my knees and then back up to my face. "I remember telling you to get on your knees, not to sit on your ass and enjoy the show." I looked up at her to see if she was serious.

Fun fact for the day. She was indeed serious.

She then looks at my hand on my cock and tilts her head to the side, contemplating what to say next. Before she could say anything else, I went ahead and stirred my pot a little more. "Oh, my bad, madam. I thought I was about to watch the show and then possibly join in. Guess I'll just sit here like a good boy and suffer in silence." I swear my smart ass mouth is going to get me in trouble, but that is a punishment I am willing to endure.

Olivia's eyebrows shoot up as soon as the sass leaves my mouth, and she shakes her head.

"Hmmm. What am I going to do with you, Alex? You are interrupting my meal over there... and that just won't do." Olivia rubs her chin, thinking of a way to make me pay for being a brat.

Her eyes light up as a plan forms in her mischievous brain. "Get up on the bed," she barks the order at me. I slowly rise to my feet and get up on the bed, sitting on the edge, waiting for her next command.

"Are we going to make this a quickie or leave all the men in my office to fend for themselves?" I look up at Olivia with a mischievous smile on my face.

"If you would keep your mouth shut, maybe we could get back down to the men in your office," she says sassily back to me.

God, I love this girl more than any words can describe.

I run my fingers over my lips to symbolize zipping them and then twisting to lock the key. She smiles at me and bends down in front of me. "Good boy, keep it up, and maybe I will let you get in on the action." She pats my cheek, then gives me a quick peck on the cheek.

When she stands back up, she points to the bed, then looks at me again.

I crawl to the headboard, the perfect spot to watch my girls play. I sit here waiting for any other words from her, hoping she lets me stay like this.

"Good, now stay," Olivia says, and I roll my eyes.

Chapter Seventeen

Olivia

I crawl up on the bed to where Rachel lies naked, spread out like a beautiful buffet, that is all for me. I make sure, as I am crawling, to admire every inch of her body, to memorize every curve and contour that is on display. It's fucking stunning, and I know a lifetime of being with her will never be long enough to appreciate it fully.

When I get to the top of the bed, I lower my face towards hers, stopping so my lips are just a breath away from hers. "Should we torture him or let him join?" I raise an eyebrow at her, waiting for an answer that I am hoping is the same as mine.

A mischievous smile creeps up onto her lips. "I think we should have a little fun, just the two of us, and let him suffer a bit." She grabs my shirt, pulls me in, and kisses me. Smashing our bodies together so there is not a single gap between us.I lift, removing my lips from hers, grab her throat, and rub my hand down her body. Descending until I get to her pussy, sliding my middle finger in just enough so that she can feel it. "Don't you dare start thinking you can run the show either. This is my show." Her eyes get big, and she nods at me eagerly.

I smile and slide my finger further into her soft heat, causing her back to arch off the bed. "There's my good girl," I whisper into her ear, bite down on her lobe, and squeeze her neck a little harder to cut off her air. "Now let me fuck you, so maybe... Just maybe... We will let Alex join in on the fun."

She tries to nod, but the pressure on her throat doesn't allow her to move.

I loosen my grip on her neck and start to kiss down her neck, making sure that I suck and nibble to mark her as mine.

Slowly, I make my way down her body, stopping at her nipple, sucking hard, and biting down, causing Rachel to yelp, then running my tongue over it to ease the sting. I lick my way over to her other nipple to bite that one also, but she pushes my head back and starts to push it down.

I look up at her and raise my eyebrow at her. "And what do you think you are doing, princess?"

She doesn't even look at me, head leaned back on the pillow, "putting your head where I need it!" She says, pushing my head harder until I finally make it to the paradise between her legs.

I kiss her beautiful pussy, then give her a slow, tor-turous lick, then blow on it. When I look up at her, she glares at me. "You need me here, princess?" I ask with a crooked grin.

"Yes, Olivia! Fucking eat your dessert already, or I will sit on Alex's face and make him do it."

"Excuse me, ma'am?" I bite her clit, causing her to gasp. "I don't think you are in any position to threaten me."

I rub my fingers across her pussy lips, spreading them apart and admiring the glistening in between. She squirms while I play with her.

I move my way back up her body, needing to feel her lips on mine. I am craving every single thing that Rachel is willing to give me right now.

This time apart has been just as torturous on me physically as it has been mentally. I can't even describe the pain in words of all that I have been dealing with, physically, mentally, and emotionally, but being right here where I am meant to be is helping all those broken pieces become less jagged.

I start to rub circles on her clit. Her breath hitches, and I giggle. "You are so responsive to me, baby." I bend down and kiss her, hard and possessively. "You are mine, he is ours, and we will never be broken apart again. Do you understand me?" I whisper against her lips as I run my tongue along the seam of her lips to gain entrance.

She nods and opens up her mouth for me, allowing me to dominate her mouth with my tongue. I slide my hand down and slowly sink my middle finger into her wet pussy again and curl it just the right way to make her back bow. Slowly pumping in and out. She moans in between short gasps. I pull out and add a second finger.

She screams out in pleasure, wrapping her hands in my hair and cementing my mouth to hers, rocking her hips against my hand.

I pump my fingers into her pussy faster as she grinds against my hand even quicker. I can feel her getting close, her walls starting to strangle my finger. The feeling is making me go feral. She finally lets go, letting the orgasm crash through her body. She screams out, and I feel a rush of liquid cover my hand.

I slowly continue to pump in and out of her, until she comes back to Earth. When the daze in her eyes disappears, I pull my fingers out and put them in my mouth, swirling my tongue around each finger to savor every last drop of the sweet taste of Rachel.

Chapter Eighteen

Rachel

Holy Fuck.

I don't know what happened to my body, but the pressure built up, and then it was like a dam broke; it felt like I pissed myself.

"I..." I can't get the word out, my cheeks are heating up, and embarrassment floods my veins.

"What..." Fuck. Words Rachel. Fucking words.

Olivia smiles at me, bends down, and gives me a passionate kiss. "You squirted, baby. It's completely normal and, in my opinion, the sexiest thing I have ever seen."

Squirting? What the fuck? I cover my face as I can feel it heating up. This is fucking embarrassing.

I feel hands wrap around my wrists and pull my hands away from my face. Olivia's face is right there when I open my eyes.

"Don't hide from me, princess. There is nothing to be embarrassed about. Nothing worth hiding from us about. We want you exactly the way you are. And I can promise you now, this is not the last time I will make you squirt. Maybe next time I can get you to do it into Alex's mouth."

My mouth drops, and I turn to look at Alex, who is staring at us with his mouth hanging wide open just as wide. Olivia turns and looks at him also. I don't think either of us was ready for the words that just came out of her mouth.

Olivia chuckles and shakes her head, placing her hand under Alex's chin to close his mouth. "Close your mouth, brat! You are going to catch flies."

I look back at Olivia. "Are we going to let him sit there and suffer or help him out?" I nod my head to his angry purple cock. That looks painful. She looks down, lets go of me, and crawls over to Alex, her sexy ass swaying with every movement.

Mmmm. I could get used to her crawling for me. She is sexy as fuck, and I can't get enough of her.

She leans over to kiss him and runs her hand down his chest. He reaches out to grab her head, but she stops him in mid-air. She grabs his wrist and pins it above his head against the headboard.

"You, sir, obviously don't know how to listen today, and I am going to enjoy every minute of your punishment for this little act right here." She is talking against his lips, and all I want to do is get in on the action, too.

"One. I am in charge here. Not you, not Rachel. ME! Got it?" He nods to her, not making a sound.

"Second. You will do as I say, or I will not let you enjoy the fun. I know Rachel's pussy is ready for you. I know I could use some relief also, but if you don't listen. You get nothing. Capeesh?"

Alex nods frantically; you can tell he is hanging on by a thread, his willpower is at the end of its limit right now, and all he wants to do is be involved, and probably cum too.

She bends down and gives him a deep, passionate kiss that makes butterflies explode in my stomach. I need to be involved, right now, so as they are kissing, I crawl up Alex's thighs and grab hold of his throbbing, hard cock. Giving it a nice squeeze, causing him to moan in Olivia's mouth.

I slowly stroke his length, then bend down and lick the pre-cum off the head, slowly lowering my mouth around him. I open my mouth wide to adjust to his size and savor all of his musky taste in my mouth. When my jaw finally starts to relax, I slowly lower my mouth down his length. He starts to move his hips to my rhythm and grabs Olivia's head to deepen the kiss. You can tell by the way he is acting that he needed this more than he is letting on. Olivia's hand starts to work its way down his chest, teasing and pulling on his nipples, while never losing his mouth. Just feeling their bodies move above mine makes me weak to the knees. I don't know how I got this damn lucky, but I will never take it for granted. These two have my heart, and I will gladly end anyone who thinks they can take what is mine again.

I pull my lips off of Alex's dick with an audible plop sound.

"Olivia, switch spots with me. I want to ride his face." She turns to look at me with a grin on her face. She must have other plans I'm not aware of.

Chapter Nineteen

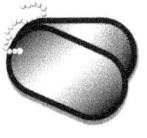

Alex

Olivia pulls her lips off mine and looks at me with a mischievous grin on her face.

"You heard our woman. She wants to ride your face. Lay down." She snaps her finger and points to the bed. I lay down without being told twice and wait for my feast to be delivered to me on a blonde, stabby platter. As soon as Rachel and Olivia move places, a leg flies over my face, and I am greeted with a beautifully glistening pussy in my face.

I grab Rachel's hips and bring her down to my face with force, refusing to waste a single second. I lick up her slit, lapping up every drop of her sweet cum on my tongue. Once I get to her clit I swirl my tongue around the sensitive nub a few times before I suck on it, causing her to moan loudly and push her pussy further into my face. That sound is an absolute symphony in my ears. Any noise these two beautiful women make, I want to record and listen to on repeat for the rest of my days.

I reach up between Rachel's legs and slide my middle finger between her slick folds, using her juices to lube up my finger before I insert it into her pussy up to the second knuckle with no warning. As soon as I feel Rachel's back bow from the intrusion, I feel Olivia penetrating herself onto my cock, until I am fully sheathed in her warm cunt.

My mind is spinning, and I can barely control the ecstasy running through my body. I wish she had given me a fucking warning, so I wasn't two seconds away from cumming.

The mix between the overpowering emotions of having Olivia back and her even willing to look at me, to me now lying here with both of my girls riding me, causes a tear to run down my cheek. These girls are my everything. There isn't a damn thing I wouldn't do for them. There is nowhere else I am meant to be; another tear runs down my cheek.

I finally get out of my head, and Olivia has picked up her speed, riding my dick like it is a mechanical bull at the bar. Rachel is rubbing her pussy all over my face, chasing any amount of friction she can get. I am just lying here in heaven with my two women using me like the slut I am for them.

I am usually the dominant one, but today, Olivia took control, and now both of my girls have power over me. I will sit here and do as they say, let them use me as they wish, and bow at their feet when they are done.

"I need both of you to cum. NOW." I say through my gritted teeth. I'm about to cum, and I need these two women to cum first.

I feel both girls clinch around me and fall over the edge, drowning me in their juices. The taste of Rachel and the feel of Olivia are so perfect. I release the tension in my body and explode into Olivia, painting her walls with everything I have.

We all fell onto the bed. A tangled pile of limbs and heavy breathing. I pull both of my girls into my arms and kiss each of their heads. My heart has never been this full.

Chapter Twenty

Rachel

This after sex bliss is one of the many things I have missed while Olivia was gone. The snuggling and just being in the arms of your people. There is no place I would rather be at this moment, but I don't know if we still have people in the office downstairs, and they probably just got a free audio-only preview of what we were doing, because I know we weren't quiet.

"We should probably go back to the office soon," I whisper. Secretly hoping they didn't hear me, so we can just stay like this for longer.

I hear Olivia sigh dramatically on the other side of Alex. "I guess we kind of have to."

"Ughhh," Alex groans before he pulls us both in tighter to his side. He starts to kiss my neck, and the scruff on his face tickles me, causing me to squirm and kick.

"Watch where you are kicking Muñeca. We don't want to break the jewels." Alex covers his junk in exaggeration.

"Oh, get over yourself. I'm not gonna kick your nuts, and even if I did, you will get over it. Don't tickle me, or you are at risk of getting kicked."

Olivia starts to get out of bed and laughs at us while I continue to squirm out of Alex's grip. "Come on, you two, we've got to go plan a war. There is no way these fuckers will threaten my girl and get away with it."

We get dressed and head back downstairs to the living room, where everyone has migrated to watch hockey on the TV. It looks like the Chicago Ice Vortex is playing against the LA Gladiators. Olivia leans over the couch and leans in close to Oliver. "Who's winning?" I guess no one heard us come down because Oliver damn near jumped out of his skin. Everyone starts to laugh, including all of Oliver's guys. "Damn, bro, didn't know a mafia boss was so easily scared?" Olivia smiles and struts her way back over to my side, grabbing my hand. Oliver was glaring daggers into her back.

"Sorry about that, gentleman. Shall we go back into the office and get to planning?" Alex claps his hands together in front of himself. You can tell he is back in full business mode, and a weight has been lifted off his shoulders. He is less doom and gloom as he walks across the living room towards his office. Oliver looks over at

Olivia and me as he turns off the TV and gets up to walk to the office; the rest of the men follow suit.

Olivia and I are the last to get into the office, our fingers intertwined. I shut the door, and everyone turns and looks at us. "Y'all got a problem with your eyeballs? I can help with that." I pull out my knife and spin it in my hands, ready to stab everyone who looks at Olivia the wrong way.

With a giggle, Olivia pulls me into her arms, pinning me in place. "Calm down, Stabby McStabberson. You're threatening the wrong people."

I roll my eyes and lean into Olivia's embrace, still playing with my knife. This knife I took from Tony has become my go-to weapon. I can't help myself; it's the perfect weight in my hand, and it's so pretty.

"Ok, gentlemen, tell me what I need to know." Alex is standing behind his desk, leaning on his hands as he looks directly at Oliver, waiting for the game plan to unfold.

"Alright, as we stated before, it seems the Starr brothers are working with the Italians. My family had no problem with them; we had previously gone to Italy and met with them. Alessio is his son, so I would assume he is in charge of the men here in the States, but I am not positive."

I feel Olivia tense up as Oliver is talking. I turn my head to see the fury in her eyes. I can only imagine what it feels like not to know about a significant part of your family until you are taken captive. I lean over and press my lips to her cheek, trying to let her know I am right here for her. She looks at me and gives me the tiniest smile. She is hurt, and I get that.

"...but as you said, Alex, your family is not friends with the Italians, so this is going to make this situation more complicated. We need to arrange for the Starr brothers not to be with the Italians when we make our moves. It's going to take some intel that I can work with you on." He nods to Alex, who returns the nod. "Then we will go in, secure them, and dispose of them."

This plan seems to be missing some details, but maybe I was distracted by Olivia when they went over it.

"How long will this take? When will we bust into action? I really just want to get this done and over with." Oliver looks at me, shocked, like I just cussed him out.

"We will be done when we are done!" He snaps, stomping toward me. Olivia pushes me down onto the couch to the side of her and stands, squaring up to her twin.

"She was asking about how long until we get this plan over with. Not when will we be done with the meeting, asshole! She is the primary target, so she has a right to these fucking questions. So calm your fucking tits or you will be dealing with me!" Olivia stares up at Oliver as he walks back a few steps.

"Sorry, Rachel, I misunderstood." Oliver's cheeks are red with embarrassment. Olivia sits back down on the couch and pulls me into her side, wrapping her arm around my shoulder protectively.

Possessively.

"All good. I just want the Starr brothers out of my life for good." He nods at me, finally understanding that I just want these fuckers gone. He then turns back toward Alex, who is now sitting in the big black chair behind his desk.

"We need to get the layout of the casino and any other information about the Italians that might help us get to the Starr brothers." Alex nods in understanding. They continue to discuss plans that I tune out, leaning into Olivia's shoulder. They will let me know when I need to do my part. As long as everything else is taken care of, I don't mind.

Chapter Twenty-One

Olivia

I am standing outside of my building, staring up at the glass windows, knowing that when I go in, I will have to get back to everything I just lived through—saving victims, stopping Lopez García and others like him. The thought of just staying at home all day makes my skin crawl. I know I don't have to be back to work, but my mind is everywhere, and I feel like I am going insane. What better way to get my mind to chill out than to put it to work?

With a deep breath, I walk through the doors, dreading every step I take further into the building.

I step into the big open office, and look around, my breath ragged, and I attempt to calm myself down. "Hey! O'Connor! Welcome back." Miller says, another officer who works in the gang unit, but I have never even spoken to him. I give him a quick wave in acknowledgment and turn back to looking at everyone getting ready for their day.

I walk up the stairs to the Captain's office to see where he wants me. It has been two weeks since I have been home, and a little over a month since I was on the dock the night my life went to shit. I was only with Lopez García for two weeks, but it felt like a lifetime. My stomach starts to turn as my mind runs through everything that happened.

Come on, Olivia. Breath.
In through your nose.
Out through your mouth.

Honestly, I'm not even sure if I want to be here anymore. I turn to walk back out the door, but my pride stops me. Dad and Oliver want me to quit, but I don't think I can. This is all I know, and they didn't trust me enough until now to include me in the family business, so why would I start now?

I turn around and continue walking forward. One step at a time. That's all it takes. I step up the three steps to the office and knock on the door.

Captain looks up from a file on his desk, and his facial expression changes to pure shock from seeing me.

"O'Connor, I wasn't expecting you back in the office so quickly after... everything that happened."

I look at him with confusion written all over my face. "With all due respect, sir, it's been two weeks. If I stay at home any longer, I might go stir crazy."

He holds up his hand to me in surrender. "Hey, I'm not complaining by any means. Glad to have you back.

Please let me know if things become too much for you. My door is always open." I nod and give my thanks while I exit the office.

"Hey, O'Connor." His voice halts me in my spot. I turn to look at him, not making a sound. "I would like you to see the staff psychiatrist and get cleared by them before I can put you on full duty again." I nod my understanding and turn to walk away.

I don't want to be put on some bullshit light-duty desk work. If they do mark me as unfit, I'll just stay home. And while I'm at it, I'll just use Alex's office to track down Lopez García myself.

As I walk back to my desk, I stop by the break room to get some coffee. Lord knows I need it today; I've only been in this office for fifteen minutes, and I'm already exhausted.

The smell of freshly brewed coffee invades my senses as soon as I enter. My stomach starts to turn, and bile rises, burning my throat. I run to the nearest trash can and throw up all of the contents in my stomach.

That was weird. I don't feel sick, and we had steak for dinner last night, so it shouldn't be food poisoning.

I grab the bag of trash and take it to the dumpster so no one knows I just puked my guts up in the break room, then come back to get my coffee. When I enter again, my stomach starts to turn from the smell.

Noted... No coffee for me today.

It's finally 5 o'clock, and I feel like I have accomplished absolutely nothing today.

Some first day back....

Everyone is already filing out of the office. I stand up to start to gather up my things, and my head starts to spin. I grab the desk with one hand and the little trashcan next to my desk and throw up the water in my stomach. That is the only thing I have been able to keep down today.

"You alright, O'Connor?" Michele, our forensics specialist, asks me.

"Yeah, I think so. Just been super nauseous today and thrown up twice so far. But I feel fine other than that. I might make an appointment with my doc to make sure it's not some virus."

"Girl, I don't want to step on toes or anything, but you might want to get a pregnancy test on your way home. This is exactly how I was with my son. Super sick, but fine other than that."

Did she just say pregnancy test? There is no way! Is there?

FUCK.

"Thanks, Michele..." My voice breaks. "I'll stop on the way home. I sure as fuck hope it's just a virus though." She laughs at my comment and starts to walk away, but I am so serious. How am I going to deal with being pregnant right now? How can I have a baby in this fucked up life I live? I just found out my dad is the head of the mafia, I am a cop who just got thrown into an auction, my boyfriend is the heir to the Cartel, and my girlfriend killed her ex... Okay, that even sounds crazy in my head. I know they are all amazing people, we just live in a fucking crazy world. Our lives are crazy.

I stop by the gas station on my way home, pick up a test, and some Skittles. I hide the test in my bag so there are no questions before I have answers. My nerves are going a thousand miles an hour right now. I don't need to have a baby... Between Lopez García and the Starr brothers, now is not the time.

When I walk in the door, the smell of cooking meat invades my nose, and once again, my stomach turns. I run upstairs into the master bathroom, slamming the door shut and locking it. I throw my bag down on the ground and barely make it to the toilet before the puke is coming up my throat and nose.

Please just be a virus.
Please just be a virus.
I hope that if I say it enough, it will be true.

I get up from the floor, grab the pregnancy test box out of my bag, wash my face, and grab my toothbrush. This taste of vomit in my mouth is going to make me puke again.

I need to take this damn test, but I really don't want to.

I brush my teeth and grab the box off the counter. My hands are shaking so bad I can't even read anything on the box.

"Well, here goes nothing," I say out loud to myself.

I open the box, ripping the whole thing to shreds with my shaking hands. The test and instructions fall on the ground in front of me. I groan. This is turning out to be more of a pain in the ass than I thought.

I bend down and pick up the test and instructions, setting the test on the counter and opening the instructions. Seems easy enough: pee on the stick, wait three minutes, and read the results. But if it's so easy, why am I hesitating? I can't even grab the test right now, my stomach is in knots, and my head is spinning.

Just do it, Olivia. You can do it. You need the answers.

When I finally get the urge to pee, I snatch the test off the counter, rip open the wrapper with my teeth, and piss on the stick. I swear this is one of the most disgusting things I have ever done. I swear I feel like I am going to pee on my hands.

When I finish, I set the test face down on the counter, so I can't see the screen. I am too scared to look. I wash my hands three times to make sure no pee is on them. I can't handle that idea right now, so I pull out my phone and set a timer for three minutes.

I start pacing the bathroom, my mind going a thousand miles an hour.

Alex would be the dad, right?
Fuck, what if it's Tony? I don't want that fuckers kid.

I shutter.

What if it's Lopez García's kid...

I start to spiral out of control with my thoughts when my alarm goes off on my phone. I freeze and turn to the test like it's the monster hiding under my bed.

Okay Olivia. You can do this. Just turn over the test.
I reach out to grab the test and freeze.
Just flip the test, Olivia.

I flip the test, two bold pink lines stare at me, taunting me, laughing at me. I feel the blood drain from my face.

FUCK.

A knock on the door scares me out of my thoughts.

"Hey, Liv, you okay? You have been in there for a while. And dinner is done." Alex's voice is soft and gentle. He has been so gentle with me since I started staying with him. I feel bad because I don't want him to feel like he has to walk on eggshells, but I am still working through my issues. Now I am just going to add another issue to the list...

Does he know what I am doing?

"Yeah... I'm okay. I'll be down in a second."

I sit down on the lid of the toilet and put my face in my hands. What will I even say to them? 'Hey guys, so I'm pregnant and I don't know who the dad is, because I got raped by the Cartel?' Yeah, that will go over well.

And what will Rachel think? I mean, she lost her baby, will she hate me because I am pregnant? Will she want me to get rid of the baby?

I throw away the test and rewash my hands before I head downstairs.

Time to face the music. I have to tell them ASAP. They will know something is up; I am terrible at lying to them.

Chapter Twenty-Two

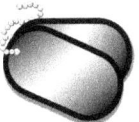

Alex

Olivia running through the house as soon as she got home was weird. I thought maybe she had to poop or something. You never know, but she was in the bathroom for a long time. When I went to check on her, I heard her breathing heavily, and it sounded like she was crying. I don't want to interrupt whatever is going on, but I also don't need her hurting herself.

I know she has been through a lot, and I refuse to lose her by her own hands if it becomes too much for her to deal with on her own. When I hear her voice through the door, my heart relaxes just a smidge.

I go back to the kitchen to finish making the salad to go with dinner. Rachel is on the couch with her face in a book, like usual. Getting that woman to put a book down has become a task in itself.

The footsteps coming down the stairs stop my thoughts, and I turn. I see a very pale Olivia, with red eyes and tear streaks down her face. My heart drops to my stomach, and next thing I know, I am running up to her, wrapping her in a hug.

"What's wrong, Azúcar?" She buries her face into my arm and shakes her head.

Well, that's not going to work. I am not taking a head shake as an answer. I put my finger under her chin and lift her head so I can look her in the eyes.

"What's going on, Azúcar? No secrets." She wipes at her eyes and nods. Then the tears start to fall again.

"I'm pregnant," she whispers against my chest.

My whole world stops. I think I stop breathing, and I stand there, holding Olivia like a lifeline.

"You are?" My voice comes out in a squeak. She doesn't seem to notice and just nods in response.

I see Rachel put her book down and walk over to join us. She grabs Olivia from behind and scoots in close.

"We got you, baby girl." Kissing the top of Olivia's head.

Olivia hiccups and looks up at me. "You aren't mad?"

"Why would I be mad, Azúcar? You are pregnant, that is nothing to be mad about." I mean that with every fiber of my being.

"But.." I cut her off with a kiss.

"No buts. You are pregnant. That's all that it is."

"But what if it's Tony's or your Grandfather's? They used me while I was with them." Her voice is so shaky, her words are barely coherent. "You don't want me... want me to get rid of it?" She is sobbing again into my shirt.

I lift her face to look at me. " Of course not, baby, I would never ask you to do that. That is your choice completely." I wrap her in a hug, trying to keep her from breaking. "And baby, what happened with Tony and my grandfather was not by your choice. Tony is dead, my Grandfather is nowhere to be found, and when he is found, he is going to be dead also. So as far as I am concerned, it's our baby." She uses her arm to wipe the tears out of her eyes and looks at me with so much love.

"It's all of our baby," Rachel says.

Olivia and I both look at her in shock.

"What? Am I not allowed to be a mommy also?" She looks at us deadpan.

Olivia looks over her shoulder and kisses Rachel. "You will always be my children's mommy."

I pull my arms out from around Olivia and wrap them around both of my girls. This is an exciting moment. I can't wait to see where this next adventure takes us.

One thing I know for sure is that these women are about to be my wives, though.

When everything calmed down, we finally got around to eating dinner. I had to warm it up because it was cold now. Then fall into bed, all of us emotionally exhausted from the day. The girls are passed out next to me, and my mind is racing, keeping me wide awake.

I wonder what the laws are in California about being married to two women? I wonder if, legally, I can only marry one. Will someone do a ceremony for the three of us? I won't marry just one.

I pull out my phone and text the only person I know who will be willing to marry me to my woman.

> **Me:** Hey, can you be my wedding officiant?

> **Xander:** dude, you are seriously fucking texting me this at 2 am?

> **Me:** Yes, I can't sleep. I need to marry these girls right now.

> **Xander:** Yeah, I can. But talk to me about it when I am actually awake.

> **Me:** Cool, thanks, bro.

Well, that's taken care of. Now to find the rings and ask them.

I finally fall asleep at around four in the fucking morning. My alarm starts to blare in my ear at six for work. Ugh, today is going to be a long day.

I get up out of bed and put on my uniform, grab my boots, and head downstairs. When I reach the bottom of the stairs, I see Olivia is already awake, sitting at the table, drinking some Orange Juice and eating some toast.

I walk up behind her and kiss her on her head.

"How did you sleep, Azúcar?"

"I slept really good. I swear, I was more tired than I have ever been in my life," She yawns.

"It's probably the pregnancy, babe. Make sure you get an appointment for the baby and let me know so I can get work off."

"Yeah! Me too." Rachel yawns from behind me, wrapping me in a hug.

"You guys want to come with me to the doctors?" The look of pure shock is adorable on her face.

"Yes, Azúcar, we are the other parents to that little Tesoro also. We will be with you every step of the way."

Rachel nods and tries to wrap us in a hug with her little arms. I back up out of the middle of the sandwich and wrap both girls in a hug. When I look at Olivia, I see tears in her eyes.

"Is someone making coffee?" Olivia's eyes get big with concern.

"Yeah, I started a cup, why?" Rachel shrugs. Olivia gets up and runs to the bedroom, holding her hand over her mouth.

"Ohhh, got it. Coffee makes her sick. Noted. I'll just have to buy coffee on the way to work from now on." Rachel giggles.

I shake my head at her and walk up the stairs to the bedroom, knocking on the bathroom door. "You okay in there?" I ask as I hear Olivia vomiting.

"Go away, Alex, you aren't going to see me like this." Little does she know that I will be here through it all.

I try to open the door, and it's locked. That just won't do. I go to the side of my bed and open my nightstand, grabbing my lock-picking kit that I always keep handy, just in case of emergencies.

I kneel by the door and open the compact kit. With steady fingers, I insert the tension wrench and pick, coaxing the lock with the delicate precision that I unfortunately learned from my grandfather. I hear the pins click softly into place, and open the door.

"ALEX! GET OUT!" Olivia yells with her face in the toilet. When she turns, I see her face is more pale than usual, and as soon as I get a glimpse of her eyes, she turns and starts puking again.

"Not happening in this lifetime. You are carrying my baby, you are sick because of my baby, and I refuse to let you go through this alone." I squat down next to her and start to rub her back, trying to comfort her.

"It might not be yours, Alex." Her eyes were full of tears again.

"Olivia Renee O'Connor, look at me. That baby is mine; I don't care whose sperm it took to conceive this baby. I will raise this baby as a García. I don't care what you say. This is my baby." I place a hand on her stomach and kiss her head.

Chapter Twenty-Three

Rachel

Pregnant.

Olivia is pregnant. My emotions are everywhere. I am not sure how to feel about it. I love that for her. I love that for us, but it makes me miss my baby. Yes, I know I told her that this baby is mine also, and it is. I will treat it as my own, but nothing will replace the baby that Andrew killed. That baby will always have a special spot in my heart.

I am sitting on the couch when I hear footsteps coming back down the stairs. I already dumped out the coffee and made sure to clean the pot so that the smell is gone.

I look over my shoulder and I see Olivia curled into Alex's arm while they walk downstairs.

"You ok, baby girl?" I ask Olivia, who looks better, but you can tell she feels like shit still.

"Yeah, I am good. I'm sorry. Apparently, the baby doesn't like coffee." She giggles. That sound is the most beautiful sound in the world.

"Well, that's going to make for a long nine months for a coffee lover like yourself." I shoot her a wink to let her know I'm playing. I remember how much my emotions were going crazy during my pregnancy.

I stand up and walk up to her when she makes it to the bottom of the steps, wrap my arms around her stomach, and drop to my knees.

"I hope you can hear me, little bean; I love you so much already. I wish I had your sibling with us, but know I will love you as my own, even if you are in your mommy's belly." When I finish my speech to the baby, I kiss her belly and look up at Olivia, who now has tears streaming down her face.

"I love you, baby, I love our little baby, and I love the family we are making. It has been a struggle, we have been through some shit, but this is home and we will make it the best home for our baby."

"Rachel, I am so sorry. I can't imagine what you're going through with me being pregnant and you having lost your baby. I am so sorry. I feel like such a shit person."

I stand up, grab her face, and kiss her as deeply and passionately as I can. I need to pour everything into this kiss to show her that this isn't her fault, and even if it was planned, I am not going to think that she is a shit person.

"Baby girl, look at me. Losing my baby wasn't your fault; it was one hundred percent Andrew's fault. Do I miss my baby? Yes, I do, deeply. But unfortunately, that baby would have had a terrible life with Andrew as its father. That baby would have seen its mommy as a weak human, as a punching bag, as a hole that gets used when their daddy wants. That's not the life I want for my baby. So, maybe it was a blessing on its own." I am now in tears also. Olivia wraps me in a hug and holds on tight.

"Your baby will always be a part of this family. It was our first baby and always will be. It just was too beautiful for this ugly Earth." Now I am sobbing from her unexpected words.

Alex walks up behind us and wraps both of us in a hug, like he always does. We both snuggle into his arms and lay our heads on his shoulders. This is my favorite spot in the whole world, in the arms of both of my people.

"I love you two," I say through a hiccup.

Olivia kisses my forehead while Alex kisses the top of my head.

"We love you, too, princess." Oliva reaches out and grabs my hand.

"Usually, people only get one person in this lifetime. How the fuck did I get so lucky to get two?" Alex squeezes us just a little tighter.

"Because each of us is the perfect missing piece to the other." I look at Olivia, "And this baby will be another piece to our puzzle."

"Alright, my beautiful women, I think we all need to get to work, or we will be late." Alex kisses our heads and then goes and grabs his keys, helmet, cover, cigarettes, and sunglasses.

"You know you are going to have to quit that nasty habit for the baby?" Olivia looks at Alex with her eyebrow arched in challenge.

"I know Azúcar." Kissing her head again. "I will quit for the baby."

These two beautiful people are the perfect pieces to my broken soul.

Chapter Twenty-Four

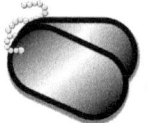

Alex

When I pull into the office parking lot, I can see that everyone is already there. Fuck, I am about to get my ass chewed out for being late.

"García, so glad you can finally join us. Want to come tell me why the fuck you are late?" Gunny nods his head to his office... Well, this is about to be fun.

I walk into his office and close the door behind me. When I turn to look at him, he is sitting down, elbows on the desk, with his fingers laced together. His brown hair is slicked back in his normal thunderbird hairstyle. I swear the guy was born in the wrong era. His brown eyes look me up and down.

"Well, get on with it." He gestures for me to sit with his hands.

"I found out one of my girlfriends is pregnant last night. And this morning, my other girlfriend made coffee, and she threw up from the smell. Well, because of all of that, we ended up having an emotional bonding moment, since my other girlfriend just went through a miscarriage from her previous relationship. So it was basically me in the middle of two emotional women this morning." I look at him with a questioning look. Waiting for the judgment, and I swear his brain glitched out.

"Wait a fucking minute...You have two girlfriends? How the fuck do you manage that? How the fuck did you even get two girls to like you, let alone date you?" He is laughing, thank god. My nerves can settle just a little.

"Well Gunny, that's a long as story, but basically, one of my girlfriends is the cop that arrested Smith that night at the bar, I went to the station to wait for her to get off to take her on a date, and then after the date, we saw my other girlfriend with her fiancé at the time getting in an argument and he kicked her into a brick building. We stopped to help her, and I ended up staying at the hospital with her that weekend, and that was that." This made his bushy brown eyebrow raise at me.

"Wow. They do say you find love in the weirdest places. I guess that must be fucking true in your case. Maybe my best friend needs to get arrested for me to find the love of my life." I raise my eyebrow back at Gunny. This dude is something else, I swear.

"Well, since I am in the office." I can hear my voice crack from the nerves running through my veins. "My reenlistment is coming up." I look up from my hands. I don't know how to say this to him.

"Your point?" I swear this man is bipolar. One minute, he is talking about finding the love of his life; the next, he is irritated with me.

"My point is, I won't be re-enlisting. I need to start getting my stuff in order to be discharged. Now that I have a baby on the way and two women at home, I don't think staying enlisted is the right choice for me." I look up from my hands. I haven't stopped fidgeting this whole time. I have not been looking forward to this conversation at all.

"I don't blame you, García, you've got a lot going on. Do you have an idea of what you want to do in the civilian world?" He is writing my name in a notepad, probably to give it to personnel so they can prepare my discharge paperwork and classes.

"I think I am going to try to take over my family business so my grandfather can rest in peace." This makes his eyes go big. He knows I hate my grandfather, he doesn't know why, but they know that my grandfather is the reason I go by only García and not the whole ass last name that is on my nameplate of my uniform. I fucking hate going by Lopez García.

Gunny stands up from his desk and stretches out his hand to me. "Well, I wish you nothing but the best of luck on your adventure."

"Thank you so much, Gunny; maybe I'll see you around." I shake his hand and leave his office.

Now, when I get home, I have to let the girls know I'm getting out, so we can find out what's going to happen next.

Chapter Twenty-Five

Olivia

I am sitting in my car for lunch break; I need to call Oliver. It's time for me to figure out the truth about why Dad never told me about my family. I am tired of the secrets, and I also need to tell him about the baby.

I pull up his contact information on my phone, and my finger hovers over the call button. Do I want to be a part of this lifestyle? I kind of already am. I am having a baby with a man who is a part of the Cartel. Sorta. I shake my head and tap the little green button before I can talk myself out of it.

"Hey, Liv! What's up?"

"Hey, we need to talk."

"Alright.. straight to the point, I guess. What's up?"

My mind is wandering. I know I need to have this conversation. I take a deep breath before I just spit out my thoughts.

"Why did you and Dad keep the family business a secret from me?"

"Damn. Okay, bringing out the big guns. Nice to hear from you too, shithead."

"Don't be a smart ass with me. I am being serious, Oliver. Why the fuck did you guys feel like I was too incompetent to know what was going on?"

"Dad didn't want you to be involved. He told me not to tell you. He didn't want you to be in danger."

"ME! IN FUCKING DANGER! I HAVE THE SAME FUCKING LAST NAME AS YOU! I AM A COP! I'M ALWAYS IN FUCKING DANGER!" My anger is boiling over. I'm more pissed off than I thought I would be.

"Damn, ok, Liv. I get it. I am just telling you what Dad said. Don't need to yell at me about it. If you want to yell at someone, yell at Dad."

"I will do whatever I damn well please, Oliver. You don't get to dictate my life. I am a grown ass woman who is about to have a kid, and I will do what is best for me and my family."

"Wait a whole ass fucking minute. A kid? Olivia, what haven't you told me?"

"I'm pregnant. I just found out yesterday."

"Is it Alex's baby?" The question makes the tears flow again.

I hiccup, "I don't know."

"It's okay, Liv. We will figure this out, even if Alex isn't the father, we will figure this out. You have options. We can take you to the clinic to have all the options laid out for you."

Is he talking about abortion? I will not be fucking aborting my baby. I don't judge people who do, but I don't have the conscience to do that.

"I will not be killing my baby. My option is to keep this baby. I am going to make an appointment with an OBGYN soon. There is no way in hell I will kill this baby. I just can't do it, Oli."

"I wasn't trying to tell you what to do, Liv. I was just saying you have options. You know I will always support your decisions, no matter what they are."

"I know, it's just.. Rachel didn't have a choice about her baby, and this is going to be our baby."

"Our?"

" Yes. Mine, Rachel's, and Alex's baby."

"Do they know?"

"Of course they know. They found out right after I did."

"And Alex is okay with it possibly not being his?"

"Alex said it may not be his biologically, but it is his."

"Good. He better step the fuck up."

"Oliver. Alex is a good guy. You know that. You are the one who told me that. You told me to hear him out."

"Yes. You are right, I am just protective of you."

"Oliver, I am fine. I am safe."

"For now..."

I roll my eyes at the phone.

"Are you still in San Diego or did you go back home already?"

"I am not going home until the Starr brothers are taken care of."

"Alright, cool. So, since our birthday already passed and we didn't get to celebrate, why don't we have dinner at my place or something?"

"Liv, that's hella random, but yeah, that sounds great."

"Cool, I'll plan it for this weekend so you can go do what you want on the actual weekend of our birthday."

"I still don't get why an almost thirty- five year old woman is obsessed with birthdays."

"Because it's our fucking day, asshole! Leave me alone and just party."

"Whatever, diva."

"Whatever, asswipe! I've got to go back to work. I'll text you later about what time to be at Alex's house."

"Alright, have fun, sis. Love you."

"Love you too. Bye."

I hang up and just stare at my steering wheel for a while. I don't know what to think about the conversation. I guess I will be dealing with the Cartel more than the Irish, since my dad is being a butt. Alex won't really have a choice if I am in his life. We are a team, and he won't be taking down Lopez García without me.

Chapter Twenty-Six

Rachel

I am deep into my work today; I have a client who is going to court next week for murder. He states it was self-defense, but the evidence does not look promising. I am reviewing all the text messages and emails. His wife was cheating on him; that part was clear, but what isn't clear is whether the lover is involved at all.

A knock on my door pulls my attention away from my case.

"Hey, you got a delivery here, love." Katie sets down the vase of mixed flowers and a small box.

Hmm, this isn't normal, but who knows, maybe it's Olivia or Alex.

I take note off the stick in the flowers to read.

Count your days.

Well, I can say that it is not from Olivia or Alex.

I set that note down next to the flower and grabbed the box. It's a small black box with a gold ribbon on it, tied in a perfect bow. Slowly, I untie the bow and open the lid of the box. I pull back the black tissue paper to reveal a stack of photos. All of them are pictures of me. When I left Andrew's apartment after killing him, sitting on the log at the beach, I was waiting for Alex, all of it.

I keep flipping through the photos, and I see pictures of me and Alex having sex, when Olivia and I were riding Alex, fuck, even Olivia and I in the kitchen. I put the photos down; I can't look anymore. I'm feeling lightheaded, and my breathing is becoming short. I know it's a panic attack happening. I haven't had one of these since I was in the hospital. I thought I was over these.

Think Rachel.

In through your nose, out through your mouth.

What are five things I can see?

My desk, a pen, my cell phone, the fucked up flowers, fuck... um... the picture on my desk.

My breathing starts to pick up pace even more. My chest is so tight. I need to call Alex.

I push the intercom, and Katie answers. I can't get a word out, and I know Katie can hear it. She comes rushing into my office.

"Rachel, are you okay?" I can only shake my head. My hand is on my chest, trying to feel my breath and attempting to calm myself down.

"Alex." That's all I get out before Katie grabs my cell phone, holds it up to my face to unlock it, and calls Alex.

"Alex, it's Katie. Something is wrong with Rachel. All she said was your name. Come to the office now. I think it might be a panic attack." She hangs up and sets my phone back down on the desk, spins my chair around, and squats in front of me.

"Look at me, Rachel. You are okay. I am right here. Breathe with me."

She leads me through the 5, 4, 3, 2, 1 method until Alex comes bursting through my door, slamming it against the wall. My breathing is better, but my chest still feels tight, and my heart is still racing.

Alex comes up to me and lifts me into his arms.

"Muñeca, are you alright?" I nod in reply.

"Yeah, I am better, thanks to Katie." He looks over at Katie, who is standing back by the door now.

"Thank you, Katie. I owe you big time. I don't know how I can repay you, but I will spend the rest of my life making this up to you. You saved Rachel, which in return means you saved me. Thank you." The panic is evident in his voice. He is freaking out over my panic attack.

Katie looks at him, completely shocked. "You don't owe me anything. I know Rachel would have done the same for me." Alex nods his head and goes back to focusing on me as Katie turns and walks out of the office.

"What happened? You haven't had a panic attack in so long. What triggered it?" I point to the flowers and the stack of photos.

Alex walks around the desk and grabs the note next to the flower. As soon as he reads it, I see him set the note down gently, but it takes every ounce of willpower not to crumble it or rip it.

When he picked up the stack of photos, his jaw tightened and teeth clenched as he continued to look through the pictures. When he finally finishes going through the pictures, he throws them down on the desk, and they go flying across the desk.

"This is bullshit! The fucking Starr brothers are going down. NOW!"

He pulls out his phone and starts to call someone.

"Oliver, we need to have a meeting tonight. We need to speed this process up." He nods on the phone while Oliver talks on the other end of the phone.

"They are sending threats to Rachel at work. This ends now."

He listens again.

"Yeah... Okay... Yeah... Bye.."

He turns back to me and sticks his hand out.

"Come on, we are going home. We have plans to make."

"You know, you make it sound like we are planning a vacation and not a war." He chuckles at my comment. I grab my briefcase off the ground, set it on the desk, and place the picture and notes in it. Grabbing Alex's hand, I walk out of the office.

This will end soon. It has to, or someone I love will get hurt.

Chapter Twenty-Seven

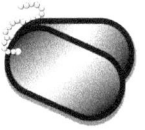

Alex

I am in my office, both girls sitting on the couch, when a rapid knock stops me from my constant thinking.

"Come in," I say while looking at the girls. Rachel, like always, is spinning a knife in one hand and the other placed on Olivia's belly protectively, looking pissed off. Olivia is leaning on Rachel's shoulder, twisting Rachel's hair around her finger, lost in thought.

Oliver walks in, nods at me, and looks over to his sister. He holds out his hand to her. She takes it willingly, stands, and wraps him in a hug. Oliver kisses the top of her head and whispers something in her ear that I can't hear. She wipes a tear from her face and hugs him harder one more time before sitting back next to Rachel.

"Alright, so let's get down to business, shall we?" Oliver claps his hands and sits in the chair in front of my desk.

Rachel sits up, leans forward, and clears her throat. "Alright, fuckers. You are looking at the wrong person. Today, while I was at work, I received a bouquet with a note in it. The note said *Count your days*. Along with the note and flowers was a small black box filled with pictures. Someone has been stalking me since Andrew's death."

I hear Olivia gasp next to her. "Why didn't you tell me?" She whispers to Rachel. I see Rachel just shake her head and go back to watching Oliver and me.

"There are a lot of things that this could mean, but first and foremost is that Rachel is getting death threats. I am not ok with one of my girls getting threatened. So the Starr brothers need to go." I make sure to keep my voice calm and stern. I don't need anyone knowing how much this situation is bothering me.

Oliver sits down in front of me. "I need to be the one to go in again; you and Rachel are too noticeable, and with Olivia being pregnant, she isn't coming."

Olivia stands up abruptly, anger flaring in her eyes. I knew before any words came out that she was pissed that Oliver wouldn't include her, but I agree with him. I will fight her on this one.

"You will not leave me out of this, Oliver!" Olivia walks up to him, puffing her chest, fists in balls at her side.

"Um, yes, the fuck I will! You are carrying my niece or nephew. You will not be putting yourself or the baby at risk!" Oliver puffs his chest back to his twin.

"Olivia, I agree with Oliver," I say to her. Her head snaps to the side, staring into my pupils with daggers that could cut diamonds.

"You have no say in what I do." She spits it out in venom.

This now spikes my temper. I can feel the tension in the air; this is about to get messy, real quick.

"You are carrying my kid, you are mine..." I point my finger at Rachel, "She is mine," then slam my hand down on the desk, "I will protect what is mine! So, don't you dare tell me no. I don't have the time or energy to deal with your stubbornness right now. You will not go into that casino, and that is final."

"Yes, the fuck I will! Either you give me a place to help, or I will go and do what I want, and it may not be what you need. So don't be a stubborn jackass and let me be fucking useful. I'm pregnant, not broken."

Fuck. What do I even say to that? She isn't wrong, but I am not backing down; she will not be going into the casino. Maybe I could put her on snipe. She could be on the lookout.

I walk around my desk and wrap Olivia in my arms, trying to keep my voice as calm as possible, not to piss her off more. I don't need my fiery red head jumping down my throat more than she already is. "You are right, Azucar, you aren't broken, but I refuse to put you or our baby in danger. Maybe you can be on the lookout or something. We will figure it out." I kiss the top of her head, and she gives a slight nod and relaxes a little in my arms.

Alright, now that that is over with, it's time to make a full, bulletproof, badass plan.

"So, I think we need to go back in and get more intel first, we need to know the Starr brothers' every move. I think this might be a part that Olivia can help with and not put herself or the baby in danger." I turn to Oliver. "What do you think?"

He looks at me for a second, turning his head to the side, observing me and thinking about what I said. Finally, he nods in agreement.

"If she goes in, so do I. I refuse to let her go anywhere alone while this shit is going on." Oliver's voice has a no shit tone to it.

"I agree completely." We both look at Olivia, who is now standing with her arms crossed across her chest and an attitude on the tip of her tongue. "Fine."

I grab her chin and make her look at me. "Listen here, Azucar, you wanted to help. You wanted to be a part of this plan; this is you being a part of it."

Chapter Twenty-Eight

Olivia

I walk into The Silver Serpent again, side by side with Oliver. This time, the hairs on the back of my neck are standing up, my pulse is racing, and I am on high alert.

I lean over to Oliver, "Let's go play some blackjack and see what we can hear from the customers and dealers. Maybe we will get some intel from the locals."

Oliver nods at me and starts walking towards the tables. We found a table close to the bar with two open seats. I sit down next to an older gentleman smoking a cigar. He has slicked-back silver hair, a tailored black Dormeuil Vanquish II suit, a red tie, and ruby-encrusted cufflinks. His cologne smells like Shumukh by Nabeel. This might be the perfect man for me to be sitting by. He is dripping in money and fancy clothes.

I am wearing an emerald green dress that falls to the floor and hugs every curve on my body just right, featuring a one-shoulder design and an overskirt with long sleeves. Oliver is wearing a Brunello Cucinelli tuxedo with an emerald green tie to match my dress. We've gotten several weird looks today because we match. But we are twins, and we enjoy matching. Everyone can suck a big fat cock if they don't like it.

My temper and attitude are at an all-time high, not only because of the pregnancy, but also the fact that I am going to see the face of the man who threatened *MY Rachel*. This situation makes me anxious, because I can't do anything besides sit here. I know I have to think of the baby, but I still want to help, be useful, and protect what is mine, but I can't.

I make myself stop thinking so much and start listening to the conversations around me. I pull out a couple of hundred-dollar bills from my black clutch bag and lay them on the table. The dealer takes the cash and hands me chips that I slide close to me. Oliver does the same to my left as the old man with slicked-back hair sits to my right, watching my every move. I give him my best flirty grin.

"Hi, I'm Olivia. What's your name?"

He starts to laugh, a deep rumble of a laugh. "Giovanni, sweet girl." His voice is deep, and he has a strong Italian accent.

I flinch at the nickname, but quickly school my features. I don't need anyone getting under my skin tonight. I feel Oliver pat my leg, and I turn to look at him. He nods to the dealer, who is intensely watching me.

"Is everyone ready?" The dealer asks, all of us nodding our heads in response.

He starts to shuffle the cards. I am assuming there are six decks to try to prevent counting cards. Little did they know, this game is my absolute favorite, and I can win no matter what.

The cards are dealt, and I look at mine. I got the queen of hearts and a jack of spades—perfect, a twenty. I then look up and start to read everyone's faces.

There is a blonde woman, wearing a red dress, sitting at the other end of the table, who lifts her eyebrows; I look at her cards, and she has a ten of spades and a seven of diamonds. Not bad. The Hispanic-looking man in a grey suit, sitting next to her, tightens his lips. I look down at his hand, a queen of diamonds and a six of spades. I bet he's thinking that if he hits, he'll go over, but if he stays, he'll lose; that's a tough call to make. The next two guys both have a forced neutral state; one has a nine of diamonds and a six of clubs. The other has a ten of clubs and a four of hearts.. That's not terrible, but they both will want to hit to have a fighting chance. Then, I look at Giovanni; he is hard to read, his face completely blank. I am more interested in what he is thinking than in what his hand is. I watch him intensely; his cards add up to eighteen, so he is fine. I look at Oliver, who raises his eyebrow, and I know he is curious to know what I think about everything. I am the twin who is good at reading people; he got all the other smarts.

The dealer nods at us, moves his card to the little viewing mirror for him to see, and nods.

"Are you guys ready?" We nod again, and he turns to the lady in the red dress.

"Hit," She says with a smirk. He flips a two of diamonds. She chews on her bottom lip, thinking hard about her next move.

"I'm going to stay," she says, waving her hands horizontally over her cards, palm down.

The Hispanic man hits. He gets a four of spades. He let out a massive sigh of relief. He got lucky as fuck.

The next guy hits and gets a king of hearts; Bust, his face drops.

The man next to him also hits and gets a ten of spades; Bust.

Now it's Giovanni's turn. He swipes his hand over the cards, and he is standing.

The dealer shifts his gaze to me and smiles. It's the first time I've really looked at him.

His smile is slimy, and it makes my stomach twist.

He looks like the kind of guy who lives in his mother's basement and spends all day gaming. His red hair is slicked back, but not in a good way; it's greasy, like it hasn't seen shampoo in weeks. Something about this guy feels off. Way off.

Then it hits me.

HE IS A STARR BROTHER!

"What will it be, sweetheart?" He raises his eyebrow at me, and I finally see all the similarities to Andrew. My fist tightened under the table.

"Stand." That's all I can say through clenched teeth. He smiles that sickening smile at me again and goes to Oliver, who also stands.

The dealer rolls over his cards, and he has a nine of hearts and a queen of spades.

"Congratulations." He says as he passes out the chips to the winners. I grab my chips, put them in my clutch, and leave the table. I need to get a drink, and it sucks because all I want is a whiskey, and I can't even have that! Fuck pregnancy. This shit is such a pain in the ass.

Chapter Twenty-Nine

Rachel

I see Olivia and Oliver walking out of Silver Serpent, and I let out a huge sigh of relief. I have been a nervous wreck the whole time they have been in there. What if one of the Starr brothers took Olivia to use her as a means to get to me? Do they even know that Olivia is affiliated with me? I mean, there are pictures of us together, but we don't know if those are actually from the Starr brothers or not. The questions keep spinning around in my head. Alex puts his hand on my thigh, shaking me out of my thoughts. "You okay?" His voice is soft.

"I am okay. Actually, no, scratch that, I am a thousand times better now that Olivia is out of that damn Casino." I say, grabbing Alex's hand and threading my fingers through his.

"I also feel like I can breathe easier, now that I see her. She doesn't realize how bad that could have gone, but I had to let her do something or else she would have been reckless, and I am not willing to risk her or the baby." I smile up at him. Look at him going all soft and papa bear–like over the little bean in Olivia's belly.

I wonder if I will ever get pregnant again. I know that I would love to have a child of my own, not that this one isn't mine, but I am not sure how Alex and Olivia will feel about it. Currently, we need to figure out how to manage the life changes that come with the growing baby in Olivia's belly, and our family of three is about to become a family of four.

I don't even know what to consider ourselves. We sleep together. Are we dating, but without the label? I have no idea. Maybe after all this shit with Tyler and his fucked up brothers is over, I will ask them what they think about the idea of us all officially dating.

"You are in your head again." Alex's fingers are under my chin, lifting my face to his. He leans in and gives me a slow, soft kiss. Just what I needed to calm my fried nerves.

"I am just thinking about Olivia and the baby and the possibility of me getting pregnant again. My mind went down that rabbit hole. I am not even sure if the miscarriage or what Andrew did fucked up my insides to the point of no return."

"Muñeca, I don't think that the miscarriage messed up your insides at all. I think that right now we need to let your body and heart heal before we decide on having a baby. But when you're healed, we will re-address this because I would love to see you pregnant with my baby." He pauses a second before a sad look appears on his face. "I hate the fact that we don't know if Olivia's is genetically ours or not."

"I don't know about you, but I am about one hundred percent sure that genetically that baby is not mine." I laugh at my own stupidity, and Alex rolls his eyes at me, a small smile forming at the corner of his lips.

"Yes, smart ass, we know it's not yours. But regardless of who the father of the baby is, he is ours."

"He? You sure about that one, big guy?"

"I have a gut feeling, but I will love it regardless if it's a boy or girl, or whose swimmers were the fastest."

My passenger side door opens, and Olivia is looking at me with a smile on her face, but it seems forced.

"So, what did you find out in there, hot stuff?" I wink at Olivia, and that makes her give me one of her radiant smiles that would bring me to my knees if I weren't already sitting in the car.

"One of the Starr brothers is the dealer at the black-jack table we were at. I don't think that he recognized us, but he did give us a slimy smile like he knew we were up to something."

"What did he look like?"

"He was a skinny redhead, hair slicked back, but it looked like it hadn't been washed in a week. He had the same slimy ass smile that Andrew did, but didn't look too much older than Andrew." I nod to what she says, going through the brothers in my head, wondering which one could be.

"Sam!" Everyone turns to look at me.

"My bad. I didn't mean to yell. I think it might be Samuel or, as the brothers call him, Sam. He is the brother who is a year older than Andrew, and they used to get mistaken for twins when they were younger. When they got older, Andrew gained weight and Sam lost it." Everyone nods at me, and then Oliver turns to Alex, discussing more plans.

I grab Olivia by the hips and bring her in between my legs, running my fingers up her arms, causing goose-bumps to cover them.

"You know what?" I say low enough for just her to hear, running my fingers over Olivia's shoulder and down into her cleavage.

"Hmm?" Olivia replies, slowly leaning her head back as I circle my fingers back to her neck.

I grab her neck and pull her face towards mine, where our noses are touching and our lips are only a breath away. "This dress would look a million times better around your ankles." Olivia's eyes widen and fill with hunger.

"And your legs would look better with my face be-tween them." She lets out a moan and starts to squeeze her legs together.

I let go of her neck and leaned back. "Too bad Alex and Oliver are here." I sigh dramatically. Olivia gets a mischievous glimmer in her eye and grabs my hand, pulling me away from the passenger seat and heading to the back of the 4Runner. She lifts the liftgate and pushes me down in the back.

She leans down to kiss me, pressing her body to mine, leaving no space between us. "You don't think that you can tease me like that, then leave me wet and needy, did you?" She raises her eyebrow, daring me to disagree with her.

I close the gap and kiss her. "I wouldn't dream of leaving my girl needy," I reply before I stand up, turn her around, pull the zipper on the back of her dress down, and slide the straps down her arm. I make sure that I touch every inch of her body as I push down her dress. When the dress is around her ankle, I kiss her thighs, and she lifts her legs to step out of the dress. When I finally have her how I want her, I push her into the back of the 4Runner.

I reach up to her waist and grab the elastic of her thong and slide it down her beautiful legs. I make a show of putting her thong in my back pocket so she knows I will not be returning it. She smiles at me with hunger in her eyes. I reach down and slide my fingers along her pussy, gathering all of her juices as I go.

I look at her wickedly and stick my fingers in my mouth, swirling my tongue around my fingers to make sure I lap up all of her juices, moaning as her taste bursts on my tongue.

"Mmm. You taste like heaven and sin wrapped up into one beautiful body." I lean in and kiss her neck, working my way down to her chest, biting her breast through the fabric of her strapless bra.

"Oh my god, Rachel, please." I smile as I make my way down her chest, pulling down her bra and licking her nipples, making sure to admire each one and leave them throbbing pebbles. I keep kissing lower to where she wants me. Her hands wrap through my hair, and she tries to push my head down to her aching core.

"Please, what baby girl? What do you want?" I slowly lick around her stomach, moving back and forth.

"I... I need..." She stutters on her words.

"Words, baby girl, I need your words." I keep licking and kissing her belly in the process, because the baby is mine, too.

"I need you, Rachel. Now!" I smile against her skin and kiss her belly one last time.

"Your wish is my command, baby." I dip my head between her legs and kiss her pretty pussy.

I have no idea what I am doing. I have never gone down on a girl, but I am just going to try to imitate what I like. If Olivia is squirming, I am probably doing it right.

I spread her lips apart and licked just a little bit to frustrate her. And just like I wanted, she growls at me.

"Remember, Baby girl, I am in control. So lie down and be a good girl." She throws her hands in the air and leans back with a groan.

I spread her open so I can clearly see her asshole, her pussy, and her clit perfectly. I do one long lick from her ass to her clit and suck her clit into my mouth. This causes her back to bow and her to moan. I rub my fingers around the entrance of her pussy and slowly slide my middle finger in, as I continue to suck on her clit.

She grabs my head and pushes me into her pussy harder. "More, I need more." If I could talk, I would tell her yes, ma'am, but my mouth is quite occupied at the moment.

I honestly thought I would hate eating pussy, I thought the taste would be weird, but honestly, Olivia's pussy is one of the sweetest things I have ever tasted, and I am enjoying making her squirm and moan. Every moan she gives me brings me closer to the edge of my own orgasm. I never thought I would be a person to get off by giving someone else pleasure, but today is a day full of surprises.

I start to lick her clit slowly, as I add my ring finger into her dripping cunt. She is wiggling around so much, I don't even know how Alex handles both of us at the same time.

I remove both of my fingers and sit up.

"What are you doing?" She is breathless, and her pupils are dilated.

"If you keep squirming so much, I won't be able to finish what I started. So as I said before, lie down and be a good girl for me." Olivia nods frantically, as if the faster she nods, the quicker I will continue what I was doing.

"Good girl," I say, and then I slam my ring and middle finger back into her pussy and lean down and kiss her, capturing her gasp in my mouth. Making sure this kiss is deep, hard, and passionate, showing all of my emotions through it. I want to worship this woman. I slowly pull my fingers almost all the way out of her and slam them back into her, causing her pussy to squeeze around my fingers. I know she is so close to the edge, and the first time I make a girl cum, it will be on my face. I want to be covered in her for the rest of the night.

I break off the kiss and go back down south to where the treasure is. I speed up my fingers and start to suck on her clit hard, adding a little nibble in there for good measure. Olivia's back arches, her pussy clenches around my fingers, and she finally moans loudly as she lets go. I bring my mouth down to where my fingers are and lick up every last drop of her cum. I will not waste a single drop of what she is willing to give me. I keep pumping my fingers in and out of her slowly until I know she comes down from her high.

When she finally relaxes under my touch, I pull my fingers out, lick them clean, and then look at her with a mischievous smile on my face. That was the best thing in the fucking world, and I get to do it as many times as I want because this girl is mine.

Chapter Thirty

Alex

I feel like the whole parking lot can hear my girls, loud and clear; if the noises are any confirmation, they are having the time of their lives, and I'm not going to tell them to stop. This shit is the hottest sex I have ever seen. I stand back and watch them from afar as Oliver goes back to Olivia's car and waits. My dick is painfully hard in my jeans right now, but I refuse to interfere with their moment.

Oliver and I were having a conversation about how to proceed next, but I kept getting distracted by the sounds of Olivia's moan and wet pussy. I could also hear Rachel telling Olivia exactly what to do. One of the sexiest things about these girls is that they aren't just submissive and not just dominant; they switch it up, and fuck does it keep things interesting.

I walk up to the girls once I see Rachel wipe her face and lick her fingers clean. "You girls have a good time?" I smile at them.

Olivia looks up at me with a smirk on her face, no shame at all. Rachel's face turns an adorable shade of red from embarrassment. I don't know what she is embarrassed about; I enjoyed every minute of the show. Watching Rachel finally take that step was honestly an honor.

"Wouldn't you like to know?" Olivia spouts off as she gets out of the back of the 4Runner, still naked from the waist down, and her tits are still hanging out of her bra. She smacks Rachel's ass as she bends down to grab her dress off the ground.

"I don't need you to tell me. The noises you were making were all the proof I need." I wink at her and walk over to her car, where Oliver is sitting, playing with his phone.

I knock on the window to get his attention, and he rolls it down and looks behind me. I see the girls now fully dressed walking up to us.

"Y'all done fucking long enough to get rid of the Starr brothers?" He says jokingly.

"Ehhh, probably not." Olivia says with a shit eating grin on her face as Rachel shoves her, giving her a look that says 'stop it.' "But long enough to make a plan."

"Fair enough, as long as I don't see my sister getting railed, I am good." Oliver opens the door and starts walking back to the front of the 4Runner, where we were originally standing.

"Alright, since the Starr brothers are working for the Italians, as far as we know, I will have to possibly reach out to some contacts I have to make it possible to get them all out of there. If we don't, we will have to take them out one by one, and that will be an invitation for retaliation. I don't know about you guys, but I would rather get this done sooner rather than later." Oliver has his phone out and is pulling up a blueprint of the casino. How he got it, I don't know.

"This is a small picture, but I have the blueprint of the casino. I think the best shot we will have is to meet up with the Italians." Oliver keeps talking, and my eyebrows shoot up. This is starting to sound like a really bad plan. I am not putting either of these girls at risk.

"Before you jump to conclusions, no one will get hurt if I have anything to do with it. I know Alessio, and I will talk to him about meeting to discuss "business" and see what other information I can get from him. I will then bring up Rachel, which should pique his interest if he is working closely with the Starr brothers." Oliver looks at his phone, closing out the blueprint and pulling up a contact. I can't read the name, but I'm assuming it's this Alessio dude.

"Are you sure about this, Oliver? Do you think he will give you the information that you want? Do you think he will be willing to help us?" Olivia's nerves are transparent just by the way she talks. Her voice is shaky; she hesitates. She is not as confident in her words as she usually is.

"Sis, I will be fine. This is not my first time being around Alessio. I..." He shakes his head before saying anything else.

"But you don't have Dad with you this time. What backup are you going to take? Especially since you two dick heads won't let me go." I raise my eyebrow and cross my arms as I look at Olivia.

"Dickheads? Really? Because we don't want anything to happen to you or the baby, we are dickheads?" I am trying to keep myself calm and neutral. I know this is her brother, and I know that she is pissed she can't help because of the pregnancy, but seriously? Calling me a dickhead?

"Yes! Y'all are being fucking dickheads! Why can't I do anything productive? I am not going to put myself or our baby at risk willingly." She starts to do that little thing where she puffs out her chest to make her seem bigger, and honestly, it takes everything in me not to laugh at her... She is a whole ass foot shorter than me. There isn't anything she can do to be bigger than me.

"Okay, okay. First off, little firecracker, can we quit calling people dickheads?" Rachel holds up her pointer finger for one.

"Second, can we please figure out who is going with Oliver and what all is going to be asked, so we have a solid game plan, because right now, this plan sounds like it's going to blow up in our faces, if I am being honest. And I will go in knives flying before I let this shit blow up in our face."

Olivier steps around the hood of the 4Runner and gets beside Olivia and me. "She is right; we need to make a foolproof plan. I may know Alessio, but it's been years since I've seen him. And... never mind." He shakes his head again and drops his eyes to the ground.

What the fuck was that about? Does Oliver have a secret we're not aware of? I am too nosey for this shit... I am about to find this out.

Chapter Thirty-One

Olivia

A couple of days later, Oliver reached out to Alessio, who agreed to have the meeting. I don't know what Oliver told him that he wanted to meet about, but whatever it was, it worked.

Today is the day, it's showtime. Oliver is in our kitchen, going over last-minute details before he goes to this meeting to hopefully get the information we need to finally fucking put a bullet in each of the Starr brothers' heads. I would be lying if I said I wasn't a paranoid wreck, and still being sick as shit from pregnancy isn't helping anything right now.

"Oliver, please be safe. You have your bracelet on you, right?" He walks around the counter and pulls me into a hug. I instantly melt in his touch. I know that he is my twin, so we are the same age, but I still worry about my brother every minute of every day.

"Liv, I never take my bracelet off." He clicks the button on the top of his bracelet, and mine glows green. It's a long-distance bracelet that has tracking devices in it. I got us when I moved out here. I don't check it often unless I feel like something is off with him. Of course, the stakeout was the first time I took it off and forgot to put it back on, and it happened to be the time I got captured. I have never taken it off since.

"I am glad you don't, because the one time I did..." Oliver grabs my face with both of his hands.

"Stop. We are not living in the past. We are O'Connors. We don't let the past dictate our future." I nod in agreement, a tear running down my cheek.

"For now." I hear Alex mumble behind us, and I can't help the cheesy smile that is now plastered on my face.

"Well, I don't see a ring on her finger. So she is still an O'Connor and will always be an O'Connor by blood." Alex shakes his head with a slight smile on his face. "I'm just giving you shit, don't bite my head off, Oliver."

Oliver turns to Alex and puts his hands on the counter, slightly leaning forward. His suit jacket hangs forward, and his red hair is styled so that only a couple of strands fall on his forehead. He looks like he's ready to attend a formal event, not just a meeting with an Italian mob boss.

Alex pulls Rachel and me to the backyard. The wind is chilly for San Diego in winter, but it's still warm for the most part outside. I mean, it's Southern California; it's always hot here, unlike back home in New York, where there's snow. I can't believe it's almost Christmas already, and I still don't know what to get anyone. Christmas has always been a very important holiday in my family. We always go big.

Alex stops in the middle of the yard and turns to us.

"I know you were not in a good place for your birthday, so we will make that up to you after all of the holidays. Your birthday is important to us, and you will not be overshadowed by Christmas or New Year's." I am looking at him, trying to figure out where he is going with this.

"But that's not why I brought you two here. While we have a few seconds of downtime, because that's all we will have, I wanted to bring you both with me to figure out some things." I am still trying to stay patient while he explains.

"Holy shit, Alex, spit it the fuck out already! I have never seen you ramble this much before." Rachel beat me to it. I have never seen Alex this nervous before.

"Fine, impatient ass. Way to make this a whole lot less memorable!" Alex turns around and walks over to the big cherry blossom tree in his backyard and bends down on one knee.

"What are you doing?" I ask, my mind going a thousand miles an hour.

"Olivia and Rachel, I met you both in the most bizarre ways possible. I didn't realize at that moment that I would catch the feelings I did." He turns and looks at me.

"Olivia, who would have thought that I would have fallen for the officer who arrested my best friend?" He then turns to Rachel, "I would have never guessed I would have been asked to stay at a hospital with a woman I didn't know, and end up falling head over heels for her." He then pulls out a big ring box and opens it.

In the box are two beautiful rings. The first one is a rose gold ring with a twisted oval ruby with white round diamonds on each side. It is incredibly gorgeous and elegant. It reminds me of Rachel so much that I start to tear up. Then it finally clicks in my head. This man is proposing to us.

The second ring is a beautiful silver band with an emerald-cut emerald halo with twisted shank. As soon as I realized that ring was for me, the flood gates opened, and I am now crying like a blubbering mess—stupid pregnancy hormones.

"Will both of you beautiful ladies be my Mrs. García?" I nod my head in response, trying to wipe the tears from my eyes. I turn to look at Rachel, who is just sitting there with her mouth wide open, completely shocked. I reach up and push her jaw closed and smile at her.

"Of all the times to propose, you choose right before a damn war?" Rachel says with a giggle. I know she's joking, but damn, she can kill the mood sometimes.

Alex stands up and walks towards her, grabbing her by the throat and pulling her chest into his. "Listen here, brat, I will propose to my women whenever the fuck I want. And that day just so happens to be today. It would have been more romantic had someone not rushed me."

I am full-on belly laughing now. These two have been bantering so much recently, and it is the funniest thing to see.

"I wouldn't have rushed you had you spit it out and stopped babbling." The sass is just flowing out of Rachel's mouth.

Alex pulls her mouth to his and kisses her hard and demanding.

There it is! He is done with her smart mouth. I am still laughing when they break off the kiss.

"So, I got my answer from Olivia through her tears. Can I please get your answer, Muñeca?" Alex's voice cracks. You can tell that he is nervous and trying to stay calm during all of this.

"Yes, Alejandro Lopez García, I will marry you." I see Alex flinch a little at the use of his full name, but he recovers quickly. He stands up, wraps Rachel in a huge hug, and spins her around. When her feet hit the ground, he turns towards me and smiles.

"Come here, Azúcar." He opens his other arm to me, and I just snuggle my way into the mix. I look up at Alex and smile at him. My heart is so full. I don't know how the three of us will get married, but we will make it happen regardless. "I love you," I whisper to him. I place my head on his chest and grab hold of Rachel to bring her closer to me. This is my family, and I will do anything for them.

Chapter Thirty-Two

Rachel

A couple of hours later, Alex gets a text from Oliver saying we need to meet up. I look down at my finger and smile at the beautiful ruby engagement ring that Alex just put there. I can't believe he asked us both to marry him. It doesn't surprise me that he would want both of us, but I am not sure how this will work. The state of California does not allow multiple people to be married to each other. I will have to do more research on this special case, because I refuse to marry just one of them. I love them both, and they are both my people. I am more complete than I have ever been.

"Hey, little Psycho, ready to kill some people?" I turn towards the voice and see that it belongs to Oliver, walking up towards me.

"I'm always ready for killing. I have been itching to use this new blade on someone. I just finished sharpening it this morning." I pull out the blade I got from Tony, twisting it side to side to admire its beauty.

"I swear, sometimes I question my sister's sanity by being with you." He shakes his head, stops next to me, and holds out his hand. "May I?" I hand him the blade and watch as he runs his fingers over the name carved into it.

"Sanchez? Your last name isn't Sanchez." I shake my head and smile up at him with a wicked smile. "Nope, but Tony's was. I took it off of him after I killed him. He doesn't deserve this beautiful work of art."

He hands me back my blade, and I gracefully put it back in its sheath at my hip. When I finally look back up, I see Oliver lost in thought; it seems like he has something serious to say.

"You okay?" I can't help but be concerned. It's Olivia's twin after all. He looks at me with a strange look in his eyes. "I never did get to thank you properly."

"Thank me for what?" The confused look on my face must have been noticeable because he came up and hugged me, taking me by surprise. I pat his back awkwardly and wait for a reply.

"Thank you for saving Olivia, and thank you for bringing her light back. Olivia has been all work and no play for as long as I can remember, and I haven't seen her smile like this since we were kids. Please don't ever let that light dim again. I can't handle my sister being sad again." Well fuck... what do I say to that?

"I don't plan on letting that light dim, and if it ever does, whoever caused it will have to answer to me." I can see his shoulder visibly relax at what I said. I suppose he still has some faith in the little psycho, after all. He turns around and goes to walk away, and without even thinking, I grab his wrist and pull him to turn towards me again.

"Hey, thank you for coming to help us at the auction. We needed you. I want you to know that I have never loved anyone as fast and hard as I love Olivia. I don't plan on leaving her ever. That woman is mine, and that baby is just as much mine as it is anyone else's. I am ready to be a mom to this baby, and I am ready to be a wife to Olivia and Alex. They are my whole life, and I will not trade our fucked up version of paradise for anything." Oliver nods and walks away again. This time, I let him leave.

Alright, Rachel. Now that Oliver has spread your emotions everywhere like fucking butter on toast, you have to get your head back in the game. It's time to end the Starr Brothers once and for all.

Chapter Thirty-Three

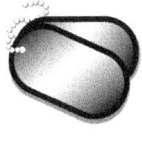

Alex

Alright, it's fucking game time.

I have Olivia on the perimeter with Oliver and some of his guys to secure the border. During Oliver's meeting, Alessio said that none of the brothers would be working tonight, and they plan to go to the underground fight club. That's where I come in. I have been underground fighting since I was a teenager. No one knows this, and I had planned not to tell anyone. I suppose I have to share my past with everyone eventually.

Oliver, Olivia, Rachel, and I pile into the 4Runner. The back is full of most of my armory from the house. When I took the girls into the hidden armory down there, Rachel's eyes went big with wonder. I swear she was like a damn kid in a candy store; she wanted to test out every gun I had in there, and man, was that a sexy fucking sight. Rachel may prefer knives, but she was a deadly shot.

I look through the rearview mirror at the blacked-out SUV driving behind us, also full of weapons and some of Oliver's men. We have at least forty men meeting us here and surrounding the perimeter. I want this kill to be ours, so they will just make sure no one gets away. I feel like the numbers are in our favor. We need to make sure that everything goes according to plan and that there are as few casualties as possible.

We pull up to the casino and drive around back. There are warehouses scattered throughout the lot that look like they would be storage. Everyone is starting to file into a single warehouse, making it clear that something is happening inside.

We park on the complete opposite side of the property from the warehouse and start to strap up. Oliver and Olivia are out, staging the men in the woods behind the Casino, and some are walking around the parking lot pretending to be security for the casino.

"Hey, how strapped up are you getting? Remember, there are rules about no guns, so we have to conceal your knives so they don't find them." I tell Rachel. She turns and looks at me like I am stupid.

"Alex, you really think I am going to get caught? I didn't even pack up my favorite knives just in case. I refuse to let someone take my stuff." I know I shouldn't have told her that. She has been extra feisty recently. If I didn't know any better, I would think that she was the one who's pregnant.

"I know. I'm sorry, I shouldn't have said anything. I am just checking every box on my list in my head a million times to make sure nothing goes wrong." I turn and look at her. She is securing a knife in her bra. "Are you sure you want to go in with me?" I see the fury flash in her eyes.

"Are you fucking serious right now, Alex? I am already pissed off enough for everyone. You really want to add comments to that? Have you forgotten I am the one they are after? Not you. Not Olivia. Not Oliver. ME." She jams her finger into her chest, emphasizing every word she says. The pain in her voice sends a knife to my heart. I know she is doing what is best for us, but I wish I could help her do more. I want to take away all of her pain and all of the treats.

"I know, baby. I know it's you, but we are a team. The three of us are a family, and you will not fight this battle, or any battle for that matter, alone." She tucks her face into my shoulder and mumbles under her breath. "Four."

"What?" The confusion was apparent in my voice.

"I said four. You said the three of us are a family. No, the four of us are a family." I tilt my head to try to process her words.

"I know Oliver is Olivia's twin, but he is more extended family." She looks up at me, pissed off, and grabs my face between her hands.

"The baby Alex. The baby is number four. Not Oliver, he is my future wife's twin. But that baby growing in Olivia's belly is ours also, a part of this family." She has a tear in her eye while she says this, and I feel like the biggest jackass there is. Of course, the baby is our family. I don't know where my mind was just at.

"I'm sorry. I don't know where my mind was at." I wipe away the tears sliding down her cheek now. "Yes, the baby is ours. Nothing will change that."

She wraps me in a hug, squeezes me tight, and then lets go. She wipes the tear from her face like it's a nuisance.

"Let's finish off these fuckers so we can go home."

I walk into the warehouse and see a makeshift rink in the center, and the crowd is packing in around it. I walk over to the edge and see that one of the Starr brothers is already bloody and pissed. If I were to guess, he just got off the mat. I walk up to the side and take off my shirt. Alessio told Oliver that it was free for all; no signing up was needed; you just got on the mat and fought. Rachel is right behind me, ready to go, but no one would know that just by looking at her. Right now, she appears to be a supportive girlfriend, but she is fully prepared to take on any of the Starr brothers.

I get into the rink and wait for my opponent to get in, too. It's another one of the Starr brothers, but he isn't nearly as big as the other one. He gets in and growls when he sees Rachel standing behind me. I turn and see her smile at him to piss him off more. I lean in and kiss

her to break their eye contact. "I need a little bit of luck."
I smile at her, and she smirks and shakes her head back
at me.

"That is good ol' Sammy boy. He is the brother who
was a year older than Andrew. He is scrappy as fuck
from what I remember Andrew saying about his fighting. He used to get into fights all the time at school." I
nod as I finish wrapping the tape around my knuckles
and turn around; it's time to get into the zone.

The crowd starts to go wild when we walk up to each
other.

"You seriously are going to protect that lying, cheating,
crazy, ugly bitch?" He snarles every word, and I let each
one sink in, letting it fuel me before I let it rain hell on
this dumb fucker.

"Hmm, I didn't know that you knew Rachel that well.
As far as I remember, it was your brother who was the
liar, and let's not forget all the bullshit he got into and
tried to sell Rachel for. He is the one who cheated, and
he was the dumbass crazy enough to kick a pregnant
woman into a fucking wall and kill their baby. It's not
my fault that she fought back, and he was too weak to
handle her." I smile at him, and I can see the war raging
in his eyes, as we circle each other. I am done talking.
This fight needs to start so I can finish off this fucker
and then his brothers.

Sam swings first, hitting me in the jaw. The entire
crowd goes wild with the first contact, signaling the
start of the fight.

There is one rule I have always had while fighting.
They only get one hit, and then they are fucked.

Chapter Thirty-Four

Rachel

I am sitting here, hands shaking as I watch every move that Alex makes; I swear, if Sam hurts him, I will lose my shit and all hell will break loose. I know that's ironic, because we are in an underground fight club. I need to make sure that no one interferes with the fight because if what Alex said was true, he would be winning this match quickly, and Sam would not be making it out of the rink at all. I pull out my phone and send a text to Olivia.

> Me: Perimeter set? Are you out of the way? Is the baby ok?

> Olivia: Holy shit, woman. I am pregnant, not fucking dying. Yes, I am fine. Yes, the baby is fine. We are ready to go when you are.

I smile at my phone because I know she is fine, but seeing her get fired up makes me giggle, and right now, I could use that. My mind starts to wander back to her, in all black, with her rifle strapped around her. It was so fucking sexy.

I know Oliver and his guys will keep her safe, because heaven fucking forbid the damn woman just stay the fuck home. I swear I was tempted to chain her ass to the bed just to make her stay at home, but Alex sided with her. Fucking pussy whipped.

I look back up and see Alex and Sam circling each other, Sam sneaking a snarling glance at me every chance he gets, and I, of course, have to give him a flirty smile and wave just to piss him off more.

After a glance at me, Sam swings and hits Alex straight in the jaw. Alex's head snaps to the side, and instantly, I see red. I grab onto the chair in front of me to stop myself from going out there and killing Sam myself. I know Alex can handle this, but it doesn't mean I have to like watching. Sam looks back at me and smiles like he just won the lottery.

Alex twists his head to crack his neck on each side and gives Sam a menacing smile. Ohhhh, he fucked up. I see the evil in Alex's eyes; the only other time I have seen this look was when we were headed to the auction to get Olivia. The Starr brothers will be lucky if all they have to do is pick up their brother off the floor and nothing worse, like scrape up his guts with a shovel.

Sam swings at Alex again but misses as Alex ducks and punches Sam right in the stomach. Sam doesn't look phased at all. He swings out his leg to try to trip Alex, another failure on Sam's part.

Alex finally steps forward and hits Sam square in the face, causing his head to snap to the side, and as soon as Sam gets his bearings, Alex hits him from the other side, sending punch after punch to Sam's face. Sam steps back, trying to get out of Alex's rapid fire, but it's no use. Alex slides his leg back and trips Sam, causing him to fall on the ground. Using the momentum, Alex does some mid-air punches, causing Sam to hit the ground harder and faster. I swear it's something that I would have seen in a movie. Once Sam is on the ground, Alex keeps hitting him, not letting up even a centimeter.

The crowd is going wild, and my eyes are focused solely on Alex. Sam is finished; he will be lucky to get out of here alive.

I am so distracted, screaming and cheering for Alex, that I don't notice the arms moving around my midsection and chest until I get pulled back, taking the breath out of my lungs. The smell of cigarette smoke and stale beer invades my senses.

I fling my head back, trying to headbutt whoever was ballsy enough to grab me, but they move out of my way, and my head hits their shoulder bone, causing them to grunt.

That grunt. I recognize it all too well. It sounds exactly like Andrew. It has to be one of his stupid brothers who has me, but I will be damned if they take me, and if they do, they will have to fight for that. He walks backwards into the crowd, dragging me with him.

"ALEX!" I scream, just before a large, rough hand clamps down over my mouth. Panic jolts through me like lightning.

Instinct takes over.

I sink my teeth into his palm, hard enough to taste blood. He jerks his hand back with a curse, but I am already thrashing, kicking, anything to get out of his grip. How fucking dare he put his hands on me?

"ALEX!" I scream a second time, trying to be heard over the crowd's noise. I feel a sharp pain in my cheek. That's when I notice that whoever the fuck has me just slapped my face, and another guy places a piece of duct tape over my mouth.

Alex turns around, searching the crowd for my voice. I see the panic rise in his eyes as soon as his eyes meet mine. He jumps out of the ring and starts running through the crowd in my direction, but no one is moving out of his way, and he is having to push and shove his way to me.

I reach my hand down towards the waistband of my pants. If I can get to my knife, I can stab this fucker and get out of their grip. The Starr brothers' arms tighten around my chest harder, pinning my arms to my side so tightly that it's starting to cut off circulation.

Alex is right behind us when we reach the door, grabbing me by my waist and pulling me towards him. The Starr brother, who is holding me, doesn't loosen his grip, and now I am basically the rope in a tug of war competition. This shit fucking hurts. I hear Alex growl, and his grip slides from my waist to my legs.

I can finally see that the Starr brother holding me is Tim, the second-oldest brother. I lean forward again and try to headbutt Tim, but this time I hit his chest and he just laughs at me. I see Nate standing to the right of Tim, watching, but not moving to help at all. Nate pushes his glasses up with a finger to the bridge of his nose, then turns around to search the crowd.

What the fuck is he even looking for?

Next thing I see, Tyler walks up with his stupid smirk on his face behind Alex. He raises his hand and the light reflects off the brass right before I could even say anything; he hits Alex in the head, and Alex crumbles to the floor. The entire room falls silent and turns to watch us. I am thrashing and screaming behind the duct tape, trying to get out of Tim's grip to get to Alex, who is now crumpled on the floor.

Tyler laughs at my attempt to get out of Tim's grip. He reaches forward to rip the tape off my lips, causing my lips to burn, but that doesn't stop me from screaming at him. "What the fuck, Tyler! Why the fuck would you do that?"

Everyone is looking at us. I'm trying to get any help, but all I'm getting are gawking eyes on me and whispers that I can't make out.

"Well, well, well. Look at the little mouse caught in the mouth of the cat—or should I say cats?" I give him a look at his stupid comment. Who even says something like that?

"What the fuck do you want with me?" I try to pull against Tim's grip, anything to get a little bit of feeling back in my arms.

"What do I want? Well, what I want is my brother to be alive, but I don't foresee you having the power to bring back the dead." He rubs his chin, looking as if he is seriously contemplating something.

He leans forward and whispers in my ear, "You know what? Maybe we can kill you." I raise an eyebrow at him. This is the worst "villain" speech I have ever heard.

"Are you done yet?" The sass rolling off my tongue, which pisses him off. Next thing I know, my head snaps to the side from the impact of Tyler's hand smacking me across the face.

"No, little murderer, I am not done. You are going to pay for what you did to Andrew." I just blink at him, waiting for him to stop talking.

"And why exactly would I do that? I told you what he did to me. I'm not going to pay for shit." I spat at him, trying to get my spit to hit him in the face.

Chapter Thirty-Five

Olivia

We have been waiting in the treeline for over an hour. My nerves will not calm down until I see Alex and Rachel come out of the building. If I weren't pregnant and next to my paranoid brother, I would have gone in already to see what was going on.

A few people have already left the warehouse. Most of them are having intense conversations as they come out. One woman came out screaming about something I couldn't hear, but her arms were flailing through the air, so it must have been intense.

"How much longer do you think it's going to take?" I ask Oliver, who is lying on the ground, his sights lined up on his sniper rifle.

"I don't know, but I am not taking my eyes off the door. I had a bad feeling about sending just the two of them in, especially Rachel. We should have sent other guys in with them." He stops talking, and his body goes rigid. I pull up my rifle and look through the scope to see what he is looking at. I see one of the Starr brothers walk out the door, but no Rachel or Alex.

"I swear to god, Olivia, if you don't put that fucking rifle down." He says without lifting his gaze. Oh my god, this man.

"Shut up, Oliver. I can shoot the rifle as long as I am safe! I looked it up." He shakes his head and goes back to watching the door.

This whole perimeter watch thing is more boring than a stakeout; at least we had shitty music in the shit mobile.

My mind starts to drift off to the day of the docks and all the people I didn't get to save, including fucking Jones. His dead body, bleeding on the dock, invades my memory. I swear I will figure out how to end these fuckers; for Jones, for the people in sex trafficking, and me.

"Olivia, I need you to stay calm, but look at the door," Oliver whispers, catching my attention. I lift my rifle and look through the scope, focusing on the door. As soon as my sight clears up, my blood turns ice cold. I see Tyler holding Rachel, being dragged out the door. My adrenaline spikes, and the only thought in my mind is 'We need to get to Rachel right now'.

"What are we going to do, because staying calm is not going to happen, and if you don't give me an order soon, I am about to get real trigger happy, real soon." I look down at Oliver, who is taking deep breaths to calm his shaking, and I see the slight movement of his trigger finger. When I look back on my sight, I see one of the Starr brothers on the ground. Tyler reaches behind himself and pulls out a blade that shines in the street light, and holds it up to Rachel's throat. You can see her say something with a smirk on her face, so I can only assume it's some smart ass comment, and Tyler looks murderous.

For the love of god, Rachel, shut your damn mouth.

"Liv, look!" Oliver says to me. When I move my sight away from Rachel, I see Alex walking out of the door, blood dripping down from his forehead, with an evil snarl on his face. He slowly walks towards Tyler, almost creeping.

"Oli, I don't know what he has planned. Keep aim on Tyler; I will aim at the other brother, next to Tyler." He grunts his approval. I position it so that it sits perfectly in the pocket of my shoulder, and take aim straight at the nerdier-looking brother. I control my breathing so that my aim never wavers.

Breathe in.
Breathe out.

Breathe in.
Breathe out.

I am ready for this fuckery to happen and be over so that I can go home.

Something shiny catches my eye, and I turn my rifle in Alex's direction. I notice a knife in his hand, but not just any knife... It looks like one of Rachel's knives.

Where did he get that? Did she drop them? Did they unarm her? I know the way that Tyler is holding her around her chest that her arms are restrained enough that she wouldn't be able to get to any of them, but that's the white one she has been obsessed with since she killed Tony.

A chill rolls down my back, and bile rises at just the thought of Tony.

I move my eyes back to the scene unfolding in front of me. Alex takes the blade and stabs Tyler right in the neck, in that artery, what the fuck is it called, Carotid artery, I think? Who knows, the fucking jugular, then sliding it across his entire throat, flaying it open wide. His blood spilling out of the gaping wound in his neck, all over Rachel. His blood is caked in her blonde hair, and it is sliding down her back, covering her shirt and pants. Her red heels now have the darker crimson of Tyler's blood sliding down them.

Rachel turns out of Tyler's grip, and before I know it, the other Starr brother is on the ground with a bullet wound to the chest. Oliver has always been a good shot, but damn, that was amazing, dead fucking center. Before I even realize what is going on, Oliver grabs my hand and runs out of the woods to where Alex and Rachel are. Rachel's hands are moving all over the place as she talks to Alex.

"The fucker hit you with brass knuckles," I hear Rachel scream at Alex as soon as I am in hearing range. He grabs her wrist in mid-air and pulls her into his embrace, kissing the top of her head.

"Are you guys ok? What the fuck happened in there?" I am running to them now, completely out of breath. They don't answer me and just open their arms, adding me to their embrace.

As soon as they close their arms around me, the world stops moving, the chaos ceases to exist, and I am home. It doesn't matter that the Starr brothers are on the ground, dead, next to us. It doesn't matter that Oliver is standing right there, watching us. Nothing matters besides Rachel and Alex. They kiss my head as Alex places his hand protectively on my belly.

"Let's call a clean-up crew and go home. I am done with today, and the only thing that will help this headache is some whiskey and pussy." Alex says.

Oliver damn near choked on his spit. "Alex, I love that you love my sister, but please don't talk about her pussy in front of me," he says, then makes a dramatic gagging sound.

"Shut up and go find Alessio. I see how you look at him. Ask pretty please, and I bet he would suck your dick." Alex shoots back at Oliver. I love that they are always joking with each other.

"You are being a smart ass while I have an AR-15 strapped to me?"

"You're going to shoot me? While your sister is so happy?"

I look over Rachel's shoulder and see Oliver roll his eyes and pull out his phone. Typing out a message to someone, then putting it back into his pocket.

"Come on..." I say, the metallic smell in the air finally makes its way to my nose, causing my stomach to start rolling. I step out of Alex and Rachel's embrace and turn to walk away, stepping on something squishy but hard. When I look down, I see Tyler's arm under my boot, and the ground is stained crimson from the blood under him. I look up from his arm that I just stepped on, moving up his body until I make it to his throat, sliced wide open, the flesh peeled back like fabric, showing every layer of muscles until you see the esophagus.

That's when everything I ate today comes right back out. I throw up so violently that I start to shake. Every ounce of throw-up lands on Tyler's face and in the gaping hole in his neck. Just that causes me to continue to throw up, and eventually, I am dry heaving. Rachel comes up behind me and starts to rub my back to comfort me.

"Please just take me home," I cry. Rachel mumbles a reply that I miss, and loops her arm through mine, pulling me away from the scene.

I have never been a squeamish person, but this pregnancy has my stomach fucked up. Being with a knife-happy woman and a trigger-happy man is going to be hard.

Chapter Thirty-Six

Alex

Oliver and I are throwing jabs back and forth, as we always do, when I see Rachel walking away with Olivia holding onto her arm. I have no clue what's going on, but I notice they are on a mission to get to the car.

"You know where they are going?" I look from the girls to Oliver, who is shaking his head.

"Olivia probably wants to go home and take a shower. She always takes a shower after throwing up and brushes her teeth. She says she feels like she just gave birth to a demon and wants to wash the dead off of her." That sounds like a very Olivia-like thing. I look back at them again, then at Oliver, trying to decide whether to go with them or help Oliver with the cleanup.

"Go. I can handle the cleanup. My sister needs you right now." I nod, not having anything to say back to him. I turn on my heels to walk towards my girls when I feel a hand pull me back.

"But since they are not here, and life isn't completely crazy right now. I want to let you know right now. My sister has been through enough hell in her life, and it took everything in her to let you back in. If you fuck up even an ounce, I will kill you, slowly, and more painfully than you could ever imagine. Olivia is my whole life. We have a special bond, and I refuse to let her get hurt after all the bullshit she has been through." The threat is clear, and the anger in his face is even more so.

"Trust me, if I hurt her, I will be crawling to your steps asking you to kill me. I don't want to lose either of these women in my life. The small amount of time that I lost Olivia is enough torture for me to never fuck up again." Oliver nods his head at me. "Go help my sister clean up. She has been a nervous wreck the whole time you guys were in the warehouse. She will need a little bit of TLC." I nod and walk off, letting all of Oliver's words run through my head, sinking deep into my soul.

All the bullshit she has been through...
Because of my family...
Should I even be with her?
Fuck

I get to the car, and Olivia and Rachel are both in the back. Rachel is running her fingers through Olivia's hair, her ruby ring glistening in the light.

"Am I a Chauffeur now?" Both girls laugh at that, and I start the car and pull out of the dirt parking lot.

"Basically, so chop, chop, and get me home. I am ready to fuck my girl." Olivia says in the back. Obviously, throwing up didn't do anything to her sassy mouth.

"Yes, ma'am," I say with a smirk and drive us home.

We get home, and Olivia immediately jumps into the shower, scrubbing her body with the loofa so hard that I am surprised she doesn't tear off her skin.

I watch her for a second before I slowly start to take off my clothes, ready to join her and let her know I am here for her, no matter what. I open the shower door and step into the inferno she calls a shower. I swear I will have to pour boiling water over myself to get my body used to the temperature of these women's showers.

"Will this water boil our baby?" I say as I grab her around the waist, feeling her jump at the contact. When she finally turns around, she locks her arms around my neck.

"No smart ass, my water will not boil the baby." I kiss the tip of her nose and smile at her. "I was only joking, Azúcar." She rolls her eyes, pulls me closer, and rests her head on my chest, swaying back and forth as if we are dancing. I sway with her, just enjoying her touch on my body. She sighs contentedly right before the door comes flying open.

"You two!" Rachel growls. We both whip around just in time to see her tearing off her clothes like they are burning her skin.

As she gets in, she says, "How could you two get in the shower together and not invite me? I love showers!" Rachel comes up behind Olivia, attempting to wrap her arms around both of us, squishing Olivia and the baby in the middle.

"In my defense, I was in the shower alone before this one here..." She jams her thumb in my direction. "Decided he had to join. I was just trying to get all the vomit off of me and brush my teeth." Rachel nods in approval and then turns her questioning gaze to me.

"So you were trying to take my girl from me?" Rachel squares her chest to me. I look down at her and raise my eyebrow... This girl is such a brat, and makes me just want to choke her and fuck her at the same time.

"And if I did?" I question her.

"Then we will have solid issues, big guy." She pokes my chest over top of Olivia's shoulder to prove a point. I reach around Olivia and grab Rachel by the neck, pushing her up against the shower wall, and move Olivia to the left side of me so I can make my point clear to Rachel, who is in charge here.

"Listen here, little girl. I will do as I please in my own house. And if you don't stop this attitude, I will make that pretty little ass of yours a beautiful shade of red, with outlines of my hand prints on it. Got it?" I make sure my voice is low and stern to get her completely at my mercy.

Rachel looks up at me for a split second, like she is contemplating everything I am saying. As soon as I see the switch in her eyes, I can tell that she is going to make my blood boil, like it's an Olympic sport.

"Ehhh, I don't think you will." She sticks out her tongue at me, and I snap. I slam my mouth down to hers, wrapping my arms around her, grabbing her hip, and spinning her so she is facing the wall. I smack her wet ass with my hand, causing the most beautiful sound to echo through the bathroom. I rub the sting with my hand and then slap the other cheek. Once I have rubbed the sting from her cheeks and watched her skin welt up with my handprint, I push my knee between her legs and make her spread her legs wide open for me. Without any warning, I slam my dick into her tight pussy, making her scream out.

"Go ahead, Brat! Scream for me. I want everyone to know who you belong to." I pull out and slam back in, causing her beautiful tits to smash against the side of the wall. I am keeping a relentless pace. I reach around and start rubbing her clit, with just enough pressure to make her go wild. The only sound in the shower right now is the sound of skin smacking against skin. I turn and look at Olivia, who is sitting on the in-shower seat watching the show with hunger in her eyes. I plan to bring her into this, but first, I have to teach our little brat a lesson.

As soon as I feel her wall tighten around me and her breathing starts to pick up, I pull out and turn around to Olivia, bending down and grabbing a fist full of her hair, pulling her head back to look directly at me, and I smash my lips to hers. I can feel the fire in Rachel's eyes on me, but I don't care. "Don't be a fucking brat, and I won't have to deny you your pleasure."

Chapter Thirty-Seven

Rachel

I turn around to see Alex standing over Olivia, his fist in her hair and his mouth on hers. Don't get me wrong, it's the sexiest sight I have ever seen. It's making the ache in my core even worse than it was when Alex pulled out of me, right as I was about to cum. Fucking bastard.

I will get him back for this.

I grab his shoulder and pull him away from Olivia, throwing him against the wall of the shower, then get down on my knees, grab Olivia's face, and slam my mouth onto hers. If he is going to deny me, then I am going to make sure to torture him also. I slowly slide my hands from Olivia's ankles and up her thighs, causing her to shudder from the soft touch of my fingers.

Alex grabs me by the back of my neck and pushes me down towards the dripping, desperate cunt between Olivia's thighs.

"Eat!" He growls in my ear, his grip tightening. "That's mine. Worship her like you're starving for it." His breath ghosts over my neck, making my skin erupt in chills.

My mouth is mere inches from her. She is soaked, trembling, and aching. Fuck, I can smell how badly she needs it, even through the downpour of water.

I turn my head and smirk at him. "Oh, I'm going to! Not because you told me to, but because she is mine, and I'm starving for her!" I sass back at him. The tick in his jaw makes the fire low in my belly spread south. I love pushing this man's nerves.

I lean down and place my hands on both of Olivia's thighs, spreading them open. Moving my hand to run my fingers through her folds, spread them open to get the most beautiful view of her dripping pussy, so needy and ready for me.

I lean in, making sure to arch my back and push my ass out to mess with Alex even more; Licking through her seam and savoring her taste that dances on my tastebuds.

I look up at her and lick my lips, "Mmm, you taste so good, baby girl," before leaning back in and rubbing my nose through her most sensitive area, making sure all my senses are overloaded with Olivia.

I run my tongue around her pussy, rimming it, before I plunge my tongue forward into her, causing a gasp to leave her mouth. The sweet sound puts a smile on my face. God, I love making Olivia lose the control she holds on to so desperately. This is the only place she allows it, so I will always take full advantage of it.

Olivia runs her hands through my wet hair, wrapping the knotted strands around her hands and pushing my face further into her cunt. I hear Alex's rumble of approval come from behind us. I assume he is watching us, but I'm not about to stop what I'm doing to give him attention. This is what he gets for denying me anything. I look up through my eyelashes at Olivia, who has a grin on her face as she stares at Alex.

Next thing I know, I am completely full, Alex is fully seated in me with one single thrust. But I refuse to make a sound to give him any satisfaction. I am not going to sit here and call him master.

Okay, I would probably call him 'master' or 'sir,' but I won't tell him that. His head is already big enough.

Alex pulls almost all the way out of me and slams back home, causing me to jerk forward and drive my face further into Olivia's sweet cunt. I keep lapping at her pussy, like a starved woman, making sure to give plenty of attention to her clit, as Alex is slamming into me relentlessly, and I can't keep myself in one spot for Olivia.

I push two fingers into Olivia's pussy. She screams out as she arches her back and reaches her hands above her, grasping at the walls of the shower, moving her hips to the rhythm Alex is setting for both of us.

Relentless.
Powerful.

Mine.

"Fuck her, Rachel, and don't you dare stop until I tell you to," Alex demands with his dom voice, I like to call it. It's his sexy lower octave voice that he uses to seduce us and demand us. It's sexy as fuck and instantly melts my insides. Another thing I will take to the grave with me.

SMACK.
Stinging erupts on my right ass cheek.
SMACK.
SMACK.

Two more smacks to my ass. I am gasping and whining into Olivia's pussy. I feel her walls tightening around my fingers, and eventually her legs start to shake. Focusing on her is the only way to keep myself from cumming.

Her grip returns to my hair, tightening and pulling at the roots. Finally, when she falls over the edge, the warm sensation of her orgasm covers my fingers. I pull out my fingers and stick them straight into my mouth. Moaning at the taste that I can't get enough of. Olivia grabs my face, squishes my cheeks, and smashes her lips to mine.

"Now it's my turn."

I have no clue what she means by that. The doggy-style position that Alex has me in will not be as easy for her to get into with the way we are positioned.

"Alex, pull out and take this to the bed." She demands, he groans as his dick slowly leaves me. Olivia's hand is in my face when I look up, reaching out to help me up. I grab it and stand up, my legs wobbling like Bambi as I stand. I look over at the bed, and Alex is already lying on it, his glare telling me that not only is he frustrated about having to pull out, but he is also getting impatient.

I smile and take this opportunity to mess with him. "Doesn't feel good to be denied, does it?" I walk towards him, putting extra sway in my step.

I climb up on the bed and turn to look at Olivia, who apparently went from the bench princess to the boss.

"Rachel, get on." She points to Alex's very erect, angry-looking cock.

"Who died and made y'all the bosses of me?" I spout off, and when I turn around to see Olivia's reaction to what I said, she is in my face with her hand wrapped around my neck.

These two sure do love to put necklaces on me.

"Listen here, princess, you're going to get up there and ride his dick, and I am going to have my turn. You've got to make me cum, now, it's my turn."

"Yes, Ma'am," I say and walk the last two steps to the bed.

Chapter Thirty-Eight

Olivia

Rachel is crawling up onto the bed next to Alex. I am ready to blow both of their minds. I don't know where these two got their brattiness from, but I am about to spank it out of both of them.

My frustration starts to rise as I watch her straddle Alex, but she makes no further moves. What the fuck is she just hovering over Alex? I tisk at her, "I said get on, not hover over the ride. So, sit yourself down, so I can begin to have my fun."

Rachel slides down until she is fully seated on Alex's cock, and I see both of their eyes roll to the back of their heads.

"Good girl." I praise, and watch Rachel shudder from a chill running down her back from my words.

"Now, Alex, put your feet on the bed and spread your legs so I can get to Rachel also." He does exactly what I commanded, which is new, because I expected a smartass comment from him.

"Alright, go ahead. I am going to watch for a second, because this view is magnificent." I walk over to the black chair in the corner of Alex's room and sit, observing every little detail that is going on. Alex's thrusts, Rachel meeting him as she slams down on him, the sounds of their slapping skin echoing through the room, the whole scene is euphoric.

They find their rhythm. Rachel's tits bouncing with each thrust, her head leaned back facing the ceiling, her full neck on display. God, I want to sink my teeth into her neck, mark her so when she goes to work, everyone knows who she belongs to.

I stand up and walk over to them, and then kneel on the bed. I start kissing up the column of Rachel's neck to her ear, nibbling just a little bit to make her body break out in goosebumps again, and then running my tongue back down.

"Mmm, and you said I taste good. Obviously, you have never tasted yourself." I whisper in her ears, she is still getting railed by Alex, the movement causing me to make sure I am just far enough away not to hurt her with my jaw into her shoulder.

I kiss my way down her back until I get down to her ass cheeks. Giving in to temptation, I take a bite of her cheek, causing her to scream out. I kiss it and work my way down even further south. I reach Alex's thigh and start kissing it, working my way up to his balls. I suck one of his balls into my mouth, causing him to freeze mid-thrust. I release it and head over to his other side to share the attention.

"Better keep going, or I will stop," I say. He immediately starts to thrust again, but this time at a slower pace. I lift his ball sack and lick my way down to his taint, licking it. I feel his body shudder, and I smile to myself. I am on a roll today, giving everyone goosebumps.

I hear Rachel cry out in ecstasy, and my smile grows wider, knowing that she has just finished, that I have finished, and now it's time to show Alex what we can actually do.

I work my way to his ass. Giving it a small lick to judge his reaction. When he doesn't freak out, or stop his now torturously slow thrusts into Rachel, I rim his ass hole some more, savoring the masculine taste of him. I keep lapping at him, making sure to leave a little extra spit there to lube him up, and I slowly push my middle finger into his ass. He jumps up at the intrusion, and his ass clenches around my finger.

"Relax, Alex," I say as I slowly pull it out and push it back in. I feel him start to relax as my finger continues to invade his space.

I just noticed that he completely stopped fucking Rachel, and she is now off of his dick and watching me with wide eyes and a hint of curiosity gleaming in them.

I raise an eyebrow at her, and she smiles, reading my mind, knowing that I am asking her to help me blow his mind.

She bends down and runs her tongue over the head of his cock before pulling the whole thing into her mouth. I hear Alex sigh, and I drop my head back to his ass, kissing his cheeks as I slowly work my finger in and out of him.

Soon, I am up to the second knuckle with my middle finger, and I start to push in the ring finger. I really want to fuck him. I want to put on my strap and ride him as he rides Rachel, but I have to get him used to the intrusion first.

"Rachel... Olivia..." He moans our names, I am assuming, trying to ask us not to stop. I start to pump my two fingers in faster, scissoring them apart as I do, stretching him wider than when I put them back together, I curl them up to hit his prostate, without warning. I feel his ass clench around my fingers, and he starts to shake. He lets out a gruntled moan, and when I look at Rachel's face, I know he is coming down her throat.

Rachel moves back, letting Alex's dick fall out of her mouth as she wipes her mouth and licks the cum off of her fingers with a moan.

"Holy hell, that was fucking intense," Alex growls, turning towards me, and I smile sweetly in return.

"What the fuck was that? What were you doing with your fingers in my ass?" He looks at me, genuinely curious. Rachel looks up towards me with questions in her eyes.

"I was stretching you out. Why?" I shrug.

"That felt fucking fantastic. But why did you do it?" Another questioning eyebrow raises at me.

"Because how else am I going to fit my dildo in your ass?" Alex starts to cough and looks at me with eyes bulging out of his head. I hold back the laugh that is threatening to escape my lips.

"What do you mean by 'dildo'?" He squeaks out. I can't help the full belly laugh that finally escapes my throat.

"I want to fuck you, Alex. I won't do it unless you agree to it, just as we agreed from the start. But the way you were rocking back on my fingers tells me that you probably would like it more than you think." I wink at him and turn to Rachel, who still looks at me completely mind-boggled from the conversation.

We all look at each other, but let the silence linger in the air with the smell of sex.

"Wait a minute." Rachel breaks the silence after a couple of seconds. "So the whole time I was sucking his dick, you were finger fucking him?" She almost looks intrigued. I nod my response.

She turns to Alex, "Did you like it?" He also nods at her.

"Fuck yes! I want to do that next!" She squeals like a kid who just got her way.

Alex looks at me with daggers. "I'm not gay!" He says with a stern voice.

Rachel turns to him with a massive smile on her face, like she is about to brat him more than usual. "No one said you were, big guy." She pats his chest and laughs.

"Don't worry, it will only be your women who get to fuck your ass, and we won't tell anyone." She bends down to kiss his cheek and smiles at him. Honestly, I thought she was going to be worse, but she isn't even really bratty at all.

He grabs her face, making her look at him. "Listen here, little girl. This mouth on you is going to get you punished!"

"You promise?" She bites her lip and laughs.

"Alright, you two, I don't know if I can handle another round. I am tired. So if you go again, have fun." I lay down on our messy, sex smelling bed, roll away from Alex and Rachel, and pass out without a second thought.

Chapter Thirty-Nine

Alex

I look over at Olivia, curled up next to us with the blanket tucked under her chin as she lets out the softest little sigh. She is completely passed out. I know I'm exhausted, and Rachel looks completely spent, too.

"Want to go downstairs, get something to eat, and maybe watch a movie?" I look over at Rachel, hoping she wants to enjoy some snuggle time also.

"Yeah, that sounds great. Let me just take a shower real quick since you ruined the last one." She spins on her heels, throws a middle finger up in the air as she walks to the bathroom, and closes the door behind her. I just shake my head and walk over to my dresser. Putting on a pair of sweatpants, then heading down to the kitchen.

Once I reach the kitchen, I pull out a beer, pop it open, and take a long swig, savoring the taste as it goes down my throat. It's been a long fucking day. And I'm ready for some normalcy in my life again.

I pull out my phone and shoot a text to Oliver.

> Me: Everything go smooth?

Oliver: Yeah, but one Starr brother isn't dead.

> Me: What the fuck do you mean not dead?

Oliver: Like still breathing?

> Me: No shit, Sherlock.

Oliver: Yeah, there are three on the ground here, and the Andrew fuck is dead, but the one you beat to a pulp in the rink is still breathing apparently, and currently at the hospital getting patched up.

What the fuck... I run my hands over my face, trying to come up with a plan to kill him off or at least get him to my fucking basement for questioning.

> Me: I'll get a guy on it.

Oliver: I'm already on it. I got a guy who knows some docs at the hospital. So he will be discharged into my custody soon.

Me: You are a fucking lifesaver, dude. Where are you taking him?

Oliver: You want him? I was going to let you choose where he goes. Obviously, I don't have a house here, I am living in Olivia's apartment that has thin ass walls.

Me: Yeah, bring him here, I've got a basement.

Oliver: On it.

I set down my phone on the counter and opened the fridge again. What the fuck am I going to cook? All I see is some lunch meat and some cheese. A sandwich it is.

I start to make the sandwiches when I hear soft footsteps coming down the stairs.

"Hey, so apparently the dude I fought isn't dead; he is in the hospital."

"Well, I guess, we should probably kill his ass before he comes after our girl again." Olivia's voice makes me jump. I was expecting Rachel. She walks up behind me and hugs me from behind, kissing my shoulder before looking to see what I am making.

"Damn, that looks good, but would be better as a grilled cheese," she whispers against my skin.

"Baby wants a grilled cheese?" I look at her, and her eyes light up like I said the magic words, and she nods. I kiss her head and turn on the stove.

"Then I guess I am making the baby a grilled cheese." I reach down and rub the tiny bump that is starting to show. No one would notice it's there, unless you knew she was pregnant.

"Thank you, Daddy." She says to me, and a tingling sensation runs down my body straight to my cock.

"I'm guessing a new kink just got unlocked?" She says with a mischievous grin.

I turn to her and grab her by the throat. "I don't know what you are playing at, but you are about to get fucked!"

"Promises, promises." She says to me as she reaches down and grabs my crotch, giving it the perfect squeeze, a groan escaping my lips. God, she knows how to fuck with me.

"Keep touching me, and I will put you up on the counter and possibly burn your grilled cheese." I raise my eyebrow as she looks at me, completely shocked that I would say such a thing.

"How dare you torture our kid like that!" she says, gasping and holding her chest dramatically.

We hear footsteps, and I turn to see Rachel coming down the stairs, a smile on her face.

"Something smells good." She comes up behind Olivia, wrapping her arms around her, centering herself, resting her hands on the baby bump. Rachel is just as obsessed with the baby as I am.

"Baby said I wanted a grilled cheese." Olivia turns and kisses her on the head.

"Make that two, Daddy, that sounds delicious. My kid has good taste!" She starts to rub the baby bump and nuzzles her face into Olivia's shoulder.

"Don't say that, Princess, you will give him a boner." Olivia laughs, and Rachel turns to me with a wicked grin.

"Oh really? Is that so? You like being called Daddy?" She walks up to me and grabs my dick, rubbing it through my sweat pants.

"Stop it or I won't finish cooking," I grumble and turn to get my dick out of her grip. These women are going to kill me.

Rachel continues to laugh as she turns around and walks back over to Olivia. "Come on, baby, let's go sit at the table." Rachel grabs Olivia's hand and leads her to the table, sitting down and pulling her onto her lap.

I finish up the grilled cheeses and hand a plate to each of my women, and take another long drag of my beer.

Olivia looks up from her sandwich, like she is waiting for me to say something. "So are you going to tell Rachel what you told me?" The question lingers in the air as Rachel looks up to me with a mouth full of grilled cheese.

"Oliver said that one of the Starr brothers isn't dead. The one I fought. What was his name again? Sam or something?"

"So where is he?" The slight tremor in her voice breaks my heart. I just want to end him for her, make it all go away.

"He is in the hospital. Oliver is getting him and bringing him here."

"Do I get to question him?" Her eyes darken with anger, but I also see a sparkle of mischief.

"Question?" I raise my eyebrow.

"Okay, Mister Specific, stab him some also." I can't help the laugh that comes out of my mouth, tears streaming down my face. I swear I'm going to pee myself laughing this hard.

"There's my girl."

Chapter Forty

Rachel

Olivia and Alex are at work, and I am stuck at fucking home alone. Since the incident with the pictures and flowers, Alex doesn't want me at the office. I have been in the office all day, trying to figure out my cases, but my mind keeps wandering back to what Alex said last night.

Sam is still alive, and he's going to be at my house. My mind continues to swirl.

What am I going to ask him? What do they want with me? Why do they work with the Italians? Fuck. This is going to be a mess. I am just hoping that I am the one causing the mess and not Sam, making a mess of my brain splattered against the floor.

A knock on the door startles me out of my spiral. I walk over and open the door. Oliver is smiling at me, holding Sam's legs, and an Italian guy is behind Oliver, holding Sam's upper body. I wonder if this is the dude Olivia mentioned.

"Who's Mister Macho behind you?" I jerk my chin to the Italian.

"Alessio, he is helping me," he says. I open the door wider to let them in.

"Go through the kitchen, and the door to the right is the basement." I give instructions as they walk through the house with an unconscious Sam.

"Where is Olivia?" Oliver yells over his shoulder as he walks toward the kitchen.

"Work. Why?" Oliver freezes at my reply. He turns his head and looks at me.

"She is still working in the gang unit?" His question is laced with concern.

"Yeah, why?"

"Because she is kinda engaged to the man who will become the drug lord. That's going to be a pain in the ass to explain to her boss."

I shrug because this whole relationship we have is kind of a mess, but it's our mess. "I mean, I am a lawyer who has killed people and am also engaged to a future drug lord, and my future brother-in-law is the future Don of the Irish mafia... I don't think any of this is how it's supposed to be, but we are just rolling with it at this point."

He nods and continues down the stairs to the basement. When they reach the bottom, I flip the light on, and there is an old, rusty metal chair covered in bloodstains in the center of the room, a metal table against the wall, and on the wall is a D hook and a chain. It reeks of rust and mildew, but I guess it's meant for torture and holding people hostage, so no point in making it smell like flowers and sunshine.

"Just tie him to the chair, I'll wait until Alex gets home to deal with him. I really don't need to be facing him alone, or we might not get any answers, but he will be dead before anyone can question him." I turn to walk back upstairs, hearing the grunts of the men doing the work that needs to be done. I am not in the mood to deal with Sam today.

I am sitting at the table when Oliver and Alessio come back up from the basement. They sit down in front of me.

"What's up? You seem lost." My nose scrunches up, and I look at him with a questionable gaze.

"I just have a lot on my mind. To start, how the fuck are we going to have a three-person wedding? That's not even legal in the state of California. Then I have my ex-fiancé's brother in my basement, tied up to a chair. My soon-to-be brother-in-law apparently just made friends with the Italians." I look to Alessio, "no offense, but I don't trust you." Alessio shrugs. He must be a man of few words. Oliver grabs my hands from across the table and looks at me with complete seriousness.

"First off, the wedding, we will figure it out. Do you want it big or small? Those details can be worked out, and we can figure out how to marry all three of you. I know that there is no other option for any of you. Now, on to Sam being in your basement. The reason we brought him here is so you get answers. If you don't want him in the house, I will kill him now and get him out of here; it's not an issue for me. The last one is Alessio. Like I said, we have known each other for a while now. I met him when my dad and I went to Italy when I was sixteen, to meet with his dad."

I see Oliver shift in his seat, and Alessio looks at him with want and longing in his eyes. Hmmm, just friends? Sure Oliver... I'm going to put a pin in this and question the fuck out of him later.

"Got it. Sorry, I associate the Italians with Andrew, and I'm not okay with anything to do with Andrew. I ended his ass for a reason, and I don't plan on ending up back in any stupid situation like that again." My head falls into my hands, and I let out a huge sigh.

Oliver stands up, walks around the table, and pulls me up to my feet. I fall into his embrace and let his warmth engulf me, and that's when the first tear falls. I wipe it away as fast as I can so no one notices, but it's too late for that.

"What's wrong? How can I help? My sister will kill me if she comes home and her fiancé is having a break-down, and I refuse to deal with her wrath when she is pregnant." Oliver lifts my face to look at him.

"I can't. I can't keep doing this." My voice cracks, and I don't even try to hold it together anymore.

"Every time someone brings up Andrew or his broth-ers, my chest tightens and I can't breathe. I live with this constant fear that it will come for me and hurt my family in the process. And now on top of all of that, I have to plan a fucking wedding!"

I let out a bitter laugh, but it died in my throat.

"I don't know how to plan a fucking wedding. I don't even know how to survive the next five minutes."

My hands start to tremble, and my chest heaves. The room starts to spin, and I grasp for the edge of the table, the wall, anything I can get my hands on.

My lungs lock up, allowing nothing to get in, and my throat starts to close. Suddenly, my air is gone.

My heart slams against my ribs like it's trying to break free, and my vision goes glassy. Black dots burst in the corners of my eyes. I blink hard to try to get them to go away, but everything is slipping out of focus.

Everything is too loud, too bright, and too fast.

I can't stop my body from shaking, and my knees buckle, but strong arms keep me upright, as the world begins to fade.

I hear Oliver's voice over the darkness. He sounds desperate, his voice echoing from the distance I can't seem to reach.

"Hey. Rachel. Look at me. Breathe. Please breathe."

But I'm gone.

Chapter Forty-One

Olivia

I just got back to my desk after getting the all clear from the psychiatrist, staring at the screen, at the faces of all the people I failed. I swear to god I will find Lopez García, if it's the last thing I do. I will search every inch of this Earth to make him pay for what he did to all these victims, what he did to me. There have been no further reports of missing persons that align with Lopez García's activities, which seems obvious given that we know he is hiding from Alex. I'm not even sure if he realizes that Alex and I are back on good terms.

My phone buzzes on my desk, ripping my attention from the screen in front of me. When I flip it, I see that it's Oliver calling. I reject the phone call, noting to call him back in a few. I am too deep into this rabbit hole to lose focus.

Not even a minute later, my phone buzzes again, and when I look, Oliver's name is flashing on the screen again. Obviously, it's important if he's calling again.

"Hey, what's up? I'm at work, looking into Lopez García."

"Yeah, I know you are at work, Rachel told me, before
she had a panic attack and passed the fuck out in my
arms."

"What do you mean, passed out in your arms?" My
voice is full of worry.

"Not like that, jackass. She was freaking out. I gave
her a hug, and next thing I know, she was hyperventi-
lating and she passed out. I am pretty sure she had an
anxiety attack. She is lying down in the master bed now,
but I can't get a hold of Alex, so I called you. Someone
needs to come home to be there when she wakes up. She
isn't in a good place, and having Sam here is messing
with her head badly."

"Fuck, okay. Let me tell someone that I have to go
home. I've got to close down everything I'm working on
real quick, I'll be home within an hour."

"Got it, be safe."

I come barreling through the front door and run to the
master bedroom. Rachel is sleeping, thank god. I broke
almost every traffic law to get here as fast as I could. Too
bad I couldn't take the cruiser home with me, I would
have had my lights on the whole damn time. When Oliver said that Rachel passed out, I was on a mission to get

home. I am not okay with my girl feeling overwhelmed when I am not here to help her. I put my fingers on her neck to check her pulse; it's strong and steady. I let out a sigh of relief.

I can't deal with this stress right now. I kiss her on her head and tuck the blanket around her, trying to make sure she is as comfortable as possible, before I head downstairs to talk to my brother.

"Hey, what's going on?" I ask as soon as I walk into the kitchen, seeing Oliver sitting next to Alessio. I raise my eyebrow in suspicion, and Oliver gives a strong jerk of his head, signaling me to shut up. Got it. Something is going on. I will figure that little tidbit out later.

"So we brought Sam to the basement, and he is tied to a chair. Rachel seemed fine until she wasn't. I thought Alex talked to you guys about this before we brought him over."

"He did. We were all on board with it, but I think Rachel didn't realize the reality of it until he was phys-ically here. I am going to go down there and wake his ass up. The sooner we get the questions answered, the better." A strong hand grabs my arm before I can step towards the stairs.

"Like hell you will." I was expecting it to be Oliver who had my arm, but the voice was not his. I turned to see the brown eyes of my furious fiancé. I noticed he was still in his uniform, with his sleeves rolled up, his muscles on display, and his helmet under his arm.

"And you are going to stop me? He has put Rachel at risk too much for him to keep breathing the same air as her."

"I agree, but you will not go down there alone." His stern voice sends a shiver down my back. I fucking love when he gets all bossy, Dom on me.

"Then come with me." I look up to him, letting him see that I am joining, whether he likes it or not.

"Fine. Are you carrying?" I look down at my uniform and look back up at him, giving him a questioning look.

"Seriously? I didn't even get out of uniform. Yes, my gun is still on me. I'm not stupid enough to go down there unprotected, regardless of whether he is tied up or not." He grunts at me and turns toward the door, my hand in his as we descend the stairs. I feel Oliver and Alessio following behind us.

Alex flips the light on, and we see Sam sitting in the metal chair, a rope tied around his chest, with each arm tied to the chair's arms. Some of his teeth are missing; I assume that's from when he fought Alex. His red hair is sticking up in every direction, greasy and unkept. I know he has been in the hospital, but he still looks like complete shit. There are stitches above his right eyebrow, and his green eyes are barely open from the swelling of his black eyes.

He finally looks up at us and smiles, "Oh, goodie, company."

"We are not the kind of company you want to be around, Sam," I say with a no-nonsense attitude. I already don't like this dude just as much as I didn't like

Andrew. I believe Rachel told me that he is the brother who was only a year older than Andrew, and they act just alike.

"Well then, Ms. Officer, what can I do for you?" The slimy smile never leaves his face.

Alex cuts in, but Sam's eyes never leave mine. "We have a few questions for you. You answer them, and this will go a lot smoother." His voice is bossy and so demanding, making my panties wet. God, I love how bossy he is, but why the fuck am I getting turned on in this situation? Fucking pregnancy hormones.

"What questions can I answer for you, soldier?"

"First off, I'm a Marine, not a Soldier. Second, stop with all of the fucking labels, it's not flattering, and it won't give you any brownie points." Sam raises his eyebrow as far as he can with the swelling.

"Why did Tyler want Rachel?" Alex barks.

"To pay back Andrew's debt," Sam says with no emotion at all.

"What debt?" Alex shoots back instantly

"Why not ask your little friend in the suit behind you? He might have some answers for you." Sam smirks, trying to divert the conversation.

"Because I am asking you, dumb fuck! If I wanted to ask Alessio, I would have already." Alex shouts.

"He had a debt with the Italians, not sure exactly what he got from them, but I knew that it was either several million in cash or they would take something important to Andrew to clear the debt."

"Something important to Andrew? And you think that was Rachel? The fucker abused Rachel. He tried to trade her repeatedly. You would have been better off giving them your mom instead of her."

Sam tries to break free from the restraints, using all his strength to escape the rope.

"FUCK!" Sam screams.

"Better luck next time, bud," Alex says as he pats Sam's cheek.

"So tell me, what else did you have planned to do with Rachel besides trade her?" Alex goes straight back to the questions. My legs are starting to hurt, so I lean up against the wall, cross my arms over my chest, and watch the exchange continue to go back and forth.

"N-nothing." Sam stutters.

"Bullshit. Were you planning on having your way with my fiancé? Just like your stupid ass brother always did?" I look at Alex. He keeps looking around the room for something. I wonder what he is looking for when he turns to me and smiles sweetly.

"Hey, babe, can you do me a favor? Can you go into the garage and grab my smaller tool bag from the bench, please? I completely forgot to grab it." His smile is oh so sweet, you wouldn't know the rage that is actually brewing in his head right now. I nod and turn around to the stairs, heading to the garage.

When I walk up to the bench, I see the tool bag. I unzip it to see what's inside. Pliers, a flat-head screwdriver, a box cutter, a drill, a hammer, wire cutters, and super-glue? I'll have to ask about the superglue; I'm not sure what he uses it for. I zip up the bag and walk back into the house and down the stairs to the basement, bag in hand with a smile on my face. I know that I am about to witness Alex letting everything out to Sam, and I am ready to see all of it.

"Hey, babe, I got your bag," I say, holding up the bag as I walk towards Alex, Oliver, and Alessio, who are all looking at me questioningly.

"What? Did I miss something?" I say with confusion, turning to look behind me to make sure no one has followed me down. The last thing I need is Rachel coming down and watching what is going on, considering she has had enough going on with her anxiety today.

Alex leans down, grabs the bag from my hand, and kisses me. "No, babe, you just look too happy bringing the bag down. I find it amusing because you know what is in the bag. You are too nosy not to look." He winks at me as I turn my gaze because I was caught red-handed snooping.

"Well, since you know that I looked in your bag, can you tell me what the super glue is for?" Alex's smile widens.

"Of course, Azúcar. As soon as Sam misbehaves, I will let you do the honors." My eyes go big at that comment. I have no idea what he does with super glue, but being the one who actually uses it sounds... fun?

I nod my head to Sam, who is just sitting there watching us like he has no care in the world.

Alex sets the bag on the ground and opens it up. As he shuffles through the bag, you can hear his groans of protest until he finds what he is looking for—the flat-head screwdriver. Hmm, interesting first choice, I can give him that. I don't think Sam will sit still for him to take off his fingernails if that's what he plans to do.

"So, Sam, do you want to tell me the truth about what you and your brothers wanted with Rachel?" As he turns around, I see that the back pocket of his pants has a pair of needle-nose pliers; I'm not sure how I missed those, and also the wire cutters in the other pocket.

"I already told you, man. We were going to give her to the Italians to pay off a debt that Andrew had, so they didn't come for us." He turns and looks at Alessio, trying to plead with him with his eyes. I turn and look to see Alessio's reaction to the comments Sam is making. Alessio turns and looks at Oliver, and shakes his head. I wonder what the fuck Oliver knows.

Oliver steps forward and grabs Sam by the shirt. His fist pulls back, then slings forward, punching him in the face. The satisfying crunch echoes through the basement. "I think it would be in your best interest to stop lying." He yells in Sam's face.

"I-I'm not lying. That's what Tyler told us to do. Get Rachel and bring her back to the Italians, that's it, that's all I know." Oliver shakes his head and motions with his hand for Alex to proceed.

Alex stalks forward and goes to grab Sam by a small part of his arm that is not covered in rope, but before Alex's hand makes contact, Sam turns and swings, catching Alex in the face with a solid hit.

My breath hitches, and I am off the wall, heading towards Alex. How the fuck did Sam just get out of the ropes? My feet stop when Alex turns and punches Sam back in the face, causing Sam to stumble back, blood now trickling down his face. As Sam is still trying to gain his bearings, Alex swings and hits Sam in the stomach. Sam buckles over and tries to catch his breath. When I see Sam slowly start to stand back up, Alex grabs his head and thrusts his knee up into Sam's face. Sam falls back onto the small bed, completely dazed, but not knocked out; he is still mumbling incoherent things.

"Oliver, Alessio, will you help me get him back in the chair? I am not sure how he got out of the rope, but it won't happen again. This fucker has gotten too many free shots on me, and I am done." I look at him, and he nods at me before heading towards the stairs. "Oh, and if he gets his hands on Olivia at all, kill him," Oliver grunts his response as he drags Sam to the chair. I roll my eyes, this mother fucker thinks that I can't handle myself.

I bend down and pick up the rope off the ground. I see the ends cut and fraying. How did he just cut that rope? I look up at Oliver, who looks down at the rope also.

He starts feeling all around Sam's body for something that he could have cut the ropes with. Finally, he pulls out a small silver razor blade that shines in the shitty lighting, from where Sam was seated. He spins it in his fingers before throwing it towards the corner of the room.

"You won't be doing that bullshit again," Oliver growls at Sam.

Alex returns to the basement a few minutes later, now out of his uniform and wearing basketball shorts and a plain white t-shirt, with several other items from his toolbox in hand. I can't tell what they are. He is whistling a tune as he walks towards the table. Oliver has Sam's hands in his grip, so nothing happens to anyone while he has some freedom.

"Oliver, keep hold of his arm while I get these zip ties around his wrist. Alessio, will you grab the other wrist for me? " Oliver and Alessio both nod. Alex sets the bag of thick black zip ties on the ground in front of Sam. He grabs a couple and starts to work on the arm that Oliver has. I turn and grab some zip ties and start on the arm Alessio is holding.

"I wouldn't do that if I were you, little O'Connor." He murmurs. I look up at him, shocked.

"Who the fuck are you calling little?" I smarted back. I am Oliver's Twin, to be exact, I am three minutes older than he is.

"Before you get your panties in a wrinkle, I am just stating the fact that Oliver is physically bigger than you." I nod, still angry, grab my zip tie, and continue to tie his wrist to the chair.

"Oh hell no, give me that!" Alex says as he grabs the zip ties from my hands.

"I can put a fucking zip tie on his wrist, Alex, I am pregnant, not broken. Look!" I make an exaggerated show about twisting my wrists and opening and closing my hands. "Everything works as it should."

Alex grabs me by my throat and brings my face only a centimeter away from his. "I know you are not broken, Azúcar, but you are pregnant with my fucking child, and I will not let the fucking Starr brothers hurt anyone else that is mine." Alex's voice is low and growly. I have to squeeze my legs together because, regardless of where we are, I am still turned on when he gets all possessive Alpha male on me.

"Yes, daddy," I say with my sweetest, most innocent voice. I hear Oliver and Alessio groan behind us. Alex growls at me like a dog, before he leans in and whispers in my ear, "Keep calling me daddy and I swear to god I will let your brother and his boyfriend take over the torture and I will be *torturing* you instead."

"Don't tease me with a good time," I swear, I love being a switch, I can be a brat and dominate. And when Alex takes control, I am more than willing to hand it over to him, but that doesn't mean I will make it easy for him to hold on to it. I am always a brat when I am not in charge.

"Are you two going to fuck, or are we going to get answers out of this asshole?" Oliver says. We break apart and turn back to Sam, who is now completely tied to the chair by his wrists and ankles, and can't go anywhere. He is slowly starting to come back to earth from the fucking beating his head just got.

"Oh, goodie, zip ties! Kinky." Sam says as his head sways from side to side.

"You know, for a man who is tied up, you talk a lot of shit."

"If I am going to die, I will die with a smart ass comment on my lips as I go." Ain't that the fucking truth.

"Alright, Sam." Alex pulls off his shirt, and I can't help the drool that leaves my mouth. I wipe my mouth and try to keep my face neutral.

"So tell me, what were you planning on doing to Rachel?" Alex asked, but Sam just turned his head away from Alex.

"You don't want to talk to me?" I grab his chin and make him look at me. "That's ok, because I have all night. I can be down here with no worry in the world. I know my girls will take care of each other." Alex walks back over to the wall and leans against it, crossing his arms, propping his foot up.

I have no idea what to do, but I need to come up with a plan to get Sam to talk and get some answers. There is only one man here who knows the other side of the story. Alessio.

Alessio has not said he was working with the Starr brothers, but I saw them together. I wonder what they were talking about.

"Hey Alessio, do you mind if we have a chat?" I jerk my head to the side towards the stairs; I would rather not have this conversation near Sam. He nods in response, then looks back at Oliver. They make eye contact for a split second before he heads up the stairs. I look over at Alex, who is still standing against the wall, his eyes on me. I smile at him and then turn, following Alessio up the stairs.

When we are in the kitchen, I close the door to the basement. "What's up?" He looks at me with soft eyes, you would never know that he is in the mafia by the way he looks on the outside. Yes, he is all hard body and sharp edges, but he is quiet and doesn't constantly wear a resting bitch face; he is usually smiling.

"When Oliver and I first went into The Silver Serpent, we saw you and some other guys sitting with the Starr brothers. Can I know what that is about?" He nods in understanding, recalling the time when we were in his casino.

"They were just asking about getting jobs at the casino to pay back Andrew's debt." Okay, so there is a debt. What debt did he owe?

"What was the debt?" He shakes his head.

"You don't want to know that. It's not pretty." This sparks my fury, and I grab him at the collar of his white button-up shirt.

"How about you don't tell me what I want to know. If it involves Rachel, then yes. I do, in fact, want to know." I spit the venom from my teeth.

"Andrew was going to give us Rachel for drugs." I blink at him, shocked. I was expecting something crazy, but that's the stupidest trade I have ever heard of.

Alessio senses the confusion and holds up his hands in surrender. "Let me explain. He told us that Rachel was going to school to become a defense lawyer. We could always use one of those on our side. He also wanted drugs, but didn't have the money for them. So he asked if we would take her for drugs, and we said yes. As you are well aware, we didn't end up taking her." I nod, my stomach is in knots. I can't believe someone would actually do that.

Scratch that. I can absolutely see Andrew doing that. "So he got the drugs?" Alessio nods at me and then starts to smooth out his shirt like he just realized that I was holding it.

"Okay, so you obviously took them up on the offer because Sam was one of the blackjack dealers the second time we came in." He nods again. Causing my fury to spike even more. I swear, people with few words irritate me.

Chapter Forty-Two

Alex

Olivia walked up with Alessio, but I prefer her being away from all of this. I doubt it will last, but I will be trying my best to get as much of this torture done before she comes back.

I turn to see Sam's head lolling from side to side. The zip ties holding his wrist are so tight that the plastic has already started to cut into his skin. Blood trickles down from the ridges. Pooling at the tips of his fingers, dripping onto the concrete floor in slow, rhythmic plinks.

I give it to Sam, he has been pretty vague with his answers, a smart ass at times, but nothing useful has come out of his mouth.

"Alright, Sammy boy, shall we let the fun begin?" I walk up to the partially conscious man. He groans in response.

"Let's see, Sam, you give me answers, and I will make this less painful for you." I smile at him with my sweetest smile.

"Bullshit," he says and then spits at me. I step back before it can hit me.

"You know, I love your fire. Too bad I have to rip it out of you." I say, patting his cheek. He tries to bite my hand, but I pull it away just in time.

I walk over to my bench full of tools to play with, and I see my cordless drill, which could be fun. I grab it off the table, snap in the 5/64" titanium bit, barely the width of a matchstick, but that made this whole thing worse. I pull the trigger and let the motor hum to life.

I turn to look at Sam, whose eyes have gone huge.

"Listen here, Sammy boy, you planned to trade my woman for a debt that your dead brother made. So we'll start small, and we earn our way up."

The drill spins, high-pitched like a dentist's tool, but colder. This is more personal. I grip his hand and press the bit against his fingernail. "This is precision work, Sammy boy, you don't want to rush it."

The bit punches through the nail plate with a crunch, then hits bone. The scream that leaves Sam's throat was instant. Blood streams down his palm as the drill stutters, caught in the marrow.

"Feel that?" I asked, "That's what control feels like."

I move on, joint by joint. Knuckle, wrist, then ankle. Each time, I choose a smaller bone and a harder target. The drill overheats and begins to whine. Blood spatters the floor in oily ribbons.

"Alright, Sam, looks like you killed my drill, so now to find a new toy to play with."

I set the drill down on the table, blood and bone dust crust the tip like rust. Sam's sobs bounce off the wall. The sound is low and raw, barely even human. I am honestly surprised he is still conscious. His head is slumped forward but still twitching like he's trying to hold on.

Fucking pathetic.

I glance back over to the tools. So many options. A blowtorch? No, that's too messy. A scalpel? Too sterile. That's when I remember the superglue in my pocket. My lips curl in an evil smile.

"Ever hear about the old KGB trick, Sam?" I ask, spinning the glue in my hand. "They used this stuff on prisoners. Sealed eyelids shut. Glued lips closed. Took days to wear off. Real poetic shit."

I crouch in front of him and flick his chin up. His eyes flutter open, red and watering.

"Wanna try a modern version?"

He whimpers, and I take that as consent. I uncork the glue with a *pop*, then reach for his hand, the same one I drilled through.

I grip the palm open. The skin is shredded, red, and swollen. I pour the glue directly into the open wound. He jerks, howling as muscles spasm as the chemicals hit raw flesh.

"Oh, I know, burns like a bitch," I murmur, holding his hand still as the glue pools, hardens, and locks his ruined hand into a stiff, mangled claw. "But it's more than pain, Sam. It's permanence."

He screams until his voice breaks, and I watch his throat work uselessly, like a fish out of water.

"Still got nine fingers left," I remind him gently, brushing hair from his blood-slick face. "And I'm just getting started."

I stand and stroll back to the table. My boots squish against the blood-smeared floor. A slow grin creeps over my face as I grab the lighter and the ice pick.

One brings fire. The other, frost. *Balance.*

When I turn back around, Sam is sobbing quietly. "Please," he croaks. "Please, I didn't know she was *yours...*"

I stop cold. "*Didn't know?*" The words echo inside me, bounce around like gunshots.

I walk up to him again, quieter this time.

"You didn't know?" I ask softly, tilting his chin again. "You were ready to sell her like she was livestock, Sam. My woman. And now, you want mercy?"

He shakes his head, but it's too late.

"You'll have to earn mercy."

I flick the lighter to life and let the flame dance just below the ice pick's tip. The metal heats slowly, glowing red.

"Let's start with your knees."

Sam starts shaking his head before I even move. His breath comes in rapid, wheezing pants, like he's trying to hyperventilate the pain away. I don't give him the luxury.

The ice pick glows dull red. I grip it like a dagger and kneel in front of him.

He starts to beg. Words slurring together, "Please," "God," "I'll talk", but I've heard it all before. Pain makes people say whatever they think will make it stop. I'm not looking for desperation. I'm looking for the truth.

I grab his right leg and slam my forearm into his thigh to pin it down. He thrashes until I drive my elbow into his kneecap. That shuts him up.

"Don't move," I growl. "You'll want this to be clean."

A lie. There's nothing clean about this.

I drive the tip of the red-hot pick into the side of his knee, just beneath the patella. Cartilage crunches like shattered glass. His scream is a broken thing, wet and animalistic. The stench of burning flesh fills the air—a sickening mix of blood, sweat, and scorched meat.

He nearly blacks out.

"Stay with me, Sam." I slap his cheek. Hard. "You pass out, I wake you up, and we start again. You understand?"

Tears streak down his cheeks as he nods frantically.

"Good."

I twist the pick. He arches up so violently that the chair tips, but it doesn't fall; his zip ties hold too tightly. His mouth hangs open, jaw trembling, no sound coming out now. Just a raw gasp like the last bit of air got ripped from his lungs.

I yank the ice pick free. Blood pours down his leg, dark and heavy.

"You're not just paying for what you thought you could do to her," I whisper, leaning close. "You're paying for all of the things your piece of shit brother did do to her."

His head lolls. I stand again and wipe the tool on a rag.

Behind me, the steel door creaks open.

I freeze.

Olivia's voice, calm and horrified all at once: "Alex..."

Shit. She hasn't seen me like this before. I have let my demons out to play.

I turn slowly. She stands there, eyes locked on me, taking in the blood on the floor, the screaming wreck of a man zip-tied to the chair, and the tools now officially all laid out on the table. She doesn't even flinch. She just stares at me, like she's seeing something she didn't expect.

Something she can't unsee.

"You weren't supposed to come back down. You were supposed to stay upstairs," I mutter, wiping my hands on a towel.

Olivia takes another step into the room, then halts. Her hand flies to her mouth.

The scent hits her fully now. Blood, sweat, piss, and that unmistakable stench of burning flesh. It clings to the walls, to the floor, to *me*.

She stumbles back a step, then doubles over, gagging. The dry heaves turn violent, and she turns away just in time to vomit against the concrete wall.

"Fuck," she whispers, her voice raw, her breathing ragged as she leans against the cold surface, wiping her mouth with the sleeve of her uniform blouse. She still hasn't changed out of her work clothes.

I stay quiet. There's nothing I can say that'll soften this.

She spins on her heel, trips over herself, and bolts. Her boots echo off the concrete as she disappears up the stairs, one hand over her mouth, the other bracing against the wall to keep from falling.

The door slams shut behind her, and the silence returns.

I stand still, staring at where she'd just been.

Then I inhale slowly through my nose, and the smell doesn't bother me anymore.

I turn back to Sam.

He's barely holding on now. Head lolled, face slick with sweat, tears, and blood. His fingers twitch like his brain is still trying to escape, but his body has already given up.

Good.

I turn to Oliver, who is still standing in the corner of the room, watching. "I'm done with him. If you want to do anything, he is all yours; if not, leave him here to die. I'll deal with it later. I need a fucking whiskey."

Chapter Forty-Three

Rachel

I wake up to the sound of Olivia throwing up downstairs. I get up and sprint down the stairs. As soon as I make it to the bathroom, I see Olivia holding onto the porcelain god. The bathroom and her uniform are covered in vomit as she continues to throw up in the toilet.

I walk in, making sure to do a little knock to let her know I am here, before I grab her hair and hold it back for her while rubbing her back. "I got you, babe," I whisper in her ear.

She groans and then starts to heave again, throwing up all of the contents of her stomach. I remember this, being pregnant and never being able to have stuff in your stomach without the baby being mad at it.

"Come on, love, let's go get you in the shower and let you brush your teeth." I grab her arm and pull her to a standing position, then grab her hand and help her up the stairs. When we enter the room, she starts to shiver uncontrollably. I sat her on the bed and walked over to the love seat to grab the throw blanket and wrap it around her.

"Stay here. I am going to start the shower." She stares down at the ground, lost in thought and not moving. I don't want to leave her alone; she looks so broken and fragile.

I start to walk backwards, making sure not to take my eyes off her, as I blindly reach for the handle of the shower, turn it on, and walk back to Olivia.

"Come on, beautiful, let's get you out of these clothes." I start to unhook the buttons on her shirt, slowly working my way down until I reach the last button, then slide the shirt off her shoulders. Then I untuck her undershirt and start to pull it over her head.

"Lift up, babe." She raises her hands, and I take off the undershirt. Leaving her in her bra and work pants. If it were any other circumstances, I would make her stay here just like this for me to admire.

"Alright, babe, I need to take off your boots and pants. Can you lift your butt so I can slide your pants down?" She nods, lifting her ass just enough so I can pull down her pants. Once they are around her thighs, she sits back on the bed, no emotions on her face. I squat down to start untying her boots, and the worry begins to eat me alive.

"Liv?" I look up, and her eyes focus on me. "Are you okay, babe?" She slowly nods her head, but looks away from me. I know she is lying to me, but about what?

"Olivia Renee!" I snap. "Tell me what's going on!"

"I was down in the basement with Alex, he was getting answers, when Sam didn't answer, Alex went off. I went upstairs to ask Alessio what the truth was. He said they made a deal with the Starr brothers; they needed a good lawyer in their corner, and the Starr brothers needed to get Andrew's debt paid off." I shiver at the mention of Andrew. I am so glad he is gone for good and can never hurt a woman again.

Olivia takes in a big breath and continues. "I also asked him about Oliver, they were seeming close, and he just kept telling me they had a past. I am not stupid, and I know something is happening now. But anyway, when we went back downstairs, the whole basement smelled of blood. I could see a hole in Sam's kneecap. Sam was saying exactly what Alessio had said, so I knew it was the truth, and when Alessio confirmed it, Alex turned and looked at me. He had a look in his eyes that reminded me of his grandfather and ripped me apart. Then the smell of the blood made my stomach turn, and I threw up in the basement, then ran upstairs to the bathroom." She sighs as I take off her second boot and sock.

"Babe, let me first off by saying that Alex loves you more than anything. The blood is something that pregnancy does not like; trust me, I wanted to throw up every time Andrew drew blood from my body. Sam's death is the best thing that will happen to our family, and Oliver will do what he needs to do." I am rubbing her hair as she is letting everything out.

I know that she needs comfort right now, and Alex is not it. I understand that the trauma of Lopez García is taking over, and I have to be her rock at this moment.

I put my hand under her chin and lifted her to look at me. "Baby, I am here for you." I bend down and kiss her.

"Rachel, don't kiss me, I was just throwing up." She shakes her head and pulls back from my hand.

"Then let's get your teeth brushed so I can kiss you all I want." She smiles at me as I grab her hand and pull her up, sliding her pants the rest of the way down her legs. She steps out of them as she looks down at me on my knees in front of her.

I smirk up at her as I kiss the inside of her thigh, then lick up to her hip. She grabs me under my arms and lifts me to stand.

"Listen here, princess. I may be mentally fucked up right now, but that won't stop me from spanking your ass for teasing me." She grabs my hair, leaning my head back to look at her.

"Then I guess you get your teeth brushed and in the shower so I can keep going, because teasing you is not on the agenda today." I reach down and grab her pussy, feeling how wet she is through her panties.

"You are so wet for me. I am ready for a taste right now." She shakes her head, seeming to be out of her head now that she has gotten it off her chest. When she walks into the bathroom, the steam from the shower fogged up the mirror, and the humidity makes my clothes feel sticky against my skin. I start to pull off my clothes as she goes to the sink to brush her teeth.

When she is done, she pulls off her bra and panties and steps into the shower, letting out a sigh as the water starts to cascade down her shoulders, going over her beautiful tits. I am standing here drooling at the sight of her perky tits growing with the pregnancy. She leans her head back and runs her fingers through her hair, and when she moans out, my control snaps.

I wrap my hand around her neck and apply the perfect amount of pressure. Her head snapped back up, eyes darkened with lust, and she grabbed my neck in return.

"I can't eat that pretty pussy if you have your hand on my neck, beautiful," I say. She smiles at me and runs her hand through my folds, slipping her finger into my entrance.

"Who said anything about eating my pussy?" She licks her lips and pulls me to her chest, causing her fingers to go deeper and a moan to slip from my mouth. She pulls my face to hers and kisses me with so much passion I feel like my knees are going to give out. I let go of her neck, grab her shoulders, and switch spots with her. I am against the wall, and I watch the wicked grin on her face get bigger with every pump of her finger.

"I don't know what made you think that you are going to be the one giving out the orgasms here."

She pulls her fingers out and sticks them in her mouth, making sure to show me as she swirls her tongue around them to get every inch cleaned off.

"You taste so good on my fingers, but you would taste even better? Your taste on my tongue." She drops to her knees, running her hands down my body as she goes, and my jaw hits the fucking floor. Holy hell, she is a fucking goddess.

When she gets in front of my pussy she smacks my legs, "Open up, princess." Without even thinking, I open up my legs wide for her and run my fingers through her hair.

She licks up my slit, stopping at my clit. She flicks it a couple of times with her tongue before she sucks it into her mouth, causing my back to bow against the cold tile and a loud moan to leave my mouth.

"Right there.. Please don't stop." I say in between moans.

"I wasn't planning on it, princess." She runs her nose between my folds and continues to feast on my pussy. Pushing two fingers in and curling them to hit the perfect spot. I start to grind against her face, grabbing onto her hair, as I feel the orgasm in me building up. My breathing starts to get ragged, and Olivia starts to pump her fingers in and out faster. My pussy starts to clench around her fingers, and my orgasm explodes out of me, covering her fingers and face.

Olivia slowly keeps pumping her fingers in and out of me and lapping up my juices as I ride the wave of my orgasm. When I finally come down, she stands back up.

"That's my good girl," she praises me, then leans in and kisses me, her tongue demanding entrance into my mouth. I open willingly, my tongue fighting hers for dominance, tasting myself on her lips. God, she is so sexy, and all mine.

I pull back and look at her. "Alright, love, let's wash up, and then we have to plan a wedding since the Starr brothers are finally taken care of." She leans in and kisses me one more time, and then grabs the loofah from behind me to wash up.

Chapter Forty-Four

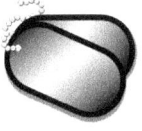

Alex

Two Months Later

I never thought about myself getting married, but here I am, in a suit and tie. Xander, to my right, is the officiant at my fucking wedding. My backyard is all decorated with fairy lights and flowers; there are chairs in the yard, and we're under the big cherry blossom tree.

Over the last two months, Xander and I have been pouring ourselves into cleaning up the backyard. Not just for the wedding, but as a way to heal. After everything we have been through, this place needed to feel like home again. The girls didn't want an expensive venue; they wanted something simple and meaningful. Just family and friends here with us on our day.

Olivia's pregnancy added another layer to all of our madness and rebuilding. Watching her move through these past weeks with strength and grace has grounded

me in ways I didn't expect. Every morning, we spend
time sanding down the old wood, hanging lights, and
planting flowers. It all feels like stitching together the
torn edges of our lives. This wasn't just a wedding. It
was about reclaiming peace, piece by piece.

The music starts to play, and my head shoots up.
We planned this wedding to be quick and intimate. We
only wanted family here. Olivia's dad is here, Oliver is
here with Alessio, my mom and siblings are here, and
Rachel's Gram is here.

When the door to the house opens, I see Olivia's dad
with both of my women walking down the aisle toward
me, ready to give them away. My eyes start to blur as
tears fill them. I'm at a loss for words. They both look
stunning.

Rachel is on August's left arm; her hair is down in
loose curls. She is wearing a beautiful, strapless, plain
white dress that hugs every beautiful curve on her body,
flowing to the ground like a mermaid's fin. I think she
mentioned it being called mermaid style or something. I
won't lie, I forgot what she said.

Olivia is on August's right arm, her hair is pinned up,
and she has a lacy white dress that stretches around her
growing belly. She is now 18 weeks pregnant, and the
little man is making his presence known.

Both of my women are glowing, and I am sitting here
starstruck by them. How the fuck did my dumbass end
up with these two beauties? The world will never know,
but I will never let them go.

"Hey buddy, are you good?" Xander whispers in my ear. I wipe the tears from my eyes and nod at him. I watch the girls, memorizing every single step they take towards our forever.

As soon as they make it to me, they are mine for good.

The reception is in full swing, and everyone is talking and dancing. Olivia is sitting down next to me, watching Rachel dance with my brother Javier. His tenth birthday was last month. We had a party for him at ma's house and made sure the wedding was far enough away not to interfere with his day.

Ever since Rachel met my family, he has been glued to her. It's the cutest thing I've ever seen. I have always been significantly older than my siblings and never got close to them, but ever since the girls went to meet my family, my siblings and I have gotten a lot closer. I feel like we are over at Ma's house every other day at this point, between the little man growing in Olivia's belly and Ma wanting to get to know the girls. It has been amazing to finally be close to my family.

Rachel finally has opened up to us about what happened to her parents, after months of us trying to get her to talk. When she was eight, she was over at a friend's house for a sleepover. There was a drive-by shooting in the neighborhood, and the generator outside her parents' house was hit, causing the house to catch fire. Their home was quickly engulfed in flames, and her parents didn't survive. She lived with her grandma until she met Andrew. Andrew's dumb fuck self made Rachel cut off Gram. That shit still pisses me off.

I look out to the crowd and see Gram swaying to the music in her seat.

"Hey, babe, I think I am going to go ask Gram to dance. Are you okay here alone?" Olivia nods to me, leaning back and rubbing her little man, you can start to see her belly jumping from him kicking her.

I get up and walk over to Gram, she looks up at me with a twinkle in her blue eye.

"May I have this dance?" I ask her. She reaches out and grabs my hand. I slowly pull her up and walk her to the makeshift dance floor in the grass. We start to sway to the music, her long, silver hair swaying in the light breeze.

I look around at all the smiling faces and see Rachel run off towards Jose, my youngest brother, who is five years old. She picks him up and spins him in a circle, both of them laughing. This is my family, and they are making it the most amazing wedding day. There is nowhere else I would rather be.

"Alejandro," a deep Italian voice calls out from behind me. I stop mid-dance and turn, pulling Gram behind me.

I see a tall man with dark brown hair and brown eyes, looking at me. "Who are you? And why are you at a private wedding?"

"Antonio?" I hear Ma say from behind me. I turn and look at her.

"You know who this is, ma?" She looks at me with sadness in her eyes. Who is this fucker, and why the fuck is my mom sad, and why is he at my wedding?

"Well, as Maria said, I am Antonio." I blink at him, waiting for him to finish.

"Ma, what the fuck is he talking about?" I rub my face with my hand, trying to get the tension out.

"I am your father, Alejandro." My world stops as I stare blankly at the man who is claiming to be my father.

"Excuse me?" I am blinking now out of sheer shock.

"I need you and Alessio to come back to Italy with me." He says like it's no big deal, and this is not my fucking wedding night.

"Absolutely not! He will not be leaving!" I hear Olivia's voice, looking over my shoulder to see her rushing over to me. I just sit here and stare at the man in front of me. I see the same brown eyes I have, I see the same nose structure, but I can tell I get most of my looks from my mom.

"He is ours!" Rachel screams out, both of my women now by my side, ready to fight anyone who dares to interrupt our peace.

That's the End for now!

About the author

Rebekah Lynn is a Navy veteran, a devoted wife, and the mother of two spirited boys who keep life adventurous and full of laughter.

Nestled in the stunning Pacific Northwest, she finds joy in the great outdoors—whether it's hiking rugged trails, camping under the stars, or simply soaking in the beauty of nature with her family.

When she's not chasing boys or braving the elements, Rebekah carves out quiet moments for herself—often with a good book in hand and a heart full of stories waiting to be told. Her writing is infused with honesty, resilience, and a deep appreciation for life's everyday magic.

Rebekah Lynn's social media links!

Acknowledgements

Thank you so much for reading He Is Ours, book two in the Lovers in Crossfire series. I hope you enjoyed the book as much as I enjoyed writing it.

As always I want to first and foremost thank my family. I don't know if I would have finish this book without your support in me. The love you show me and telling me how I can do it means the world to me. Thank you for always being my cheerleaders.

Then I need to give a huge shout out to Tori! Girl, for how many times I have called you, needing your help processing something in my brain or needing your input on if something sounds stupid or not. You are the reason this book is the way it is. Your support and friendship has meant the world to me and I hope you know you are forever stuck with me.

Next is Haleigh. You are so much more than just my PA, you are such a great friend and all of the challenges you have battled with me through this book. Pushing me beyond my limits and motivating me beyond words. You always bring me back when I stray away. You are seriously more than what I could ask for. Thank you for always having faith in me.

Finally I would like to thank my Beta Readers! Natasha and ChaChi! You guys are absolutely amazing! Thank you for reading my book and giving me all the feedback to make it what it is! You guys are super stars and appreciate you more than I can express!

www.ingramcontent.com/pod-product-compliance
Lightning Source LLC
Chambersburg PA
CBHW071559110726
47908CB00007B/2164